JULIAN DICKERSON
AND THE
HIGHER UPS

Copyright © 2021 Jo Ferrone
All rights reserved. No part of this book may be reproduced or used in any manner without the prior written permission of the copyright owner, except for the use of brief quotations in a book review.
To request permissions, contact the publisher at info@lifetopaper.com
Hardcover: 978-1-777-3736-8-9
Ebook: 978-1-7773736-9-6
First paperback edition November 2021.
Edited by Tabitha Rose & Flor Ana Mireles
Cover art by
Life to Paper Publishing Inc.
Toronto, Canada | Miami, U.S.
www.lifetopaper.com
Disclaimer: This book is a work of fiction. All of the characters, organizations and events portrayed in this story are either products of the author's imaginations or used fictitiously.

JULIAN DICKERSON
AND THE
HIGHER UPS

JO FERRONE

CHAPTER
One

J ulian Lenon Rainflower Dickerson only ever used the first and last of his names. He considered the rest to be ridiculous, keeping with everything else his mother and father (if father he was) ever produced out of the strawberry fields of their addled brains. Julian had no known siblings, but suspected many halves were likely disseminated across God's good earth. The sexual promiscuity of commune living made this almost a certainty. We do not choose our parents, but neither, in this case, did the parents feel they had any choice in the selection of their son. He was popped out quite painlessly and two full months before he was due in a makeshift hot tub that, for the occasion, was surrounded by half a dozen marveling communal passersby. This scenario may have precipitated Julian's tendency to be physically modest in the extreme. In any event, he didn't get this quality from his mother. During his gestation, little Julie-to-be had ingested cloud masses of pot and a variety of other drugs and may therefore have come to the conclusion, very early in his life, that he had had quite enough. It didn't pass his attention that his parents for certain had their surfeit and that not he nor anyone else could persuade them of the fact.

By the time he was five, Julian was more of a disciplinarian to his parents than they ever were to him, which was kind of a downer for all concerned. It wasn't unexpected, when as a teenager, Julian carefully packed his small belongings and set off to find a more compatible place in the world. It's not that he had no love for his relatives and the other members of the community nor that they had ever rejected him, he simply never was and never would be a good fit.

Happily, for him, he found his grandparents on his mother's side who resided in Westchester, NY, and whom he had never met, to be quite as conservative as he was. For themselves, Grandmother and Grandfather marveled at the fact that such a well-mannered, sensible boy could have sprung from the womb of their profligate daughter. They attributed this miracle to God and were happy to introduce their young grandson to the Christian ideals his very character bore witness to. They acted in every way (as a matter of duty more than of affection) as the parents Julian never really had, and he was completely content to play the role of model son. To his great comfort, there was such a thing as normal, and he had finally found it. Yet, there remained the one thing that no human or even nonhuman power could serve to mitigate. Julian had arrived at his grandparents' doorstep all of five foot two inches tall and he would say his goodbyes several years later, standing at exactly the same less-than-adequate height. And even if the young man himself had been okay with this, it was forever clear that the world at large was not.

Julian couldn't help but favor the students who were shorter than him. Yes, there was still time for them to grow, but, at age thirteen, who could say? His preppy attire was intended to blend in, but he made certain it was dissimilar enough to the student uniform that he wouldn't be mistaken for one of them instead of the distinguished English teacher he had worked so hard to become. Driving several towns over to purchase the elements of his standard wardrobe and to do so at a proper Brooks Brothers store in the boy's rather than the men's department was a worthwhile hedge against embarrassing encounters.

He knew how it was for the smaller freshmen. Without question, they were teased and bullied and tossed around like dog toys.

"If I give them a better grade," Julian thought, "then I'm tipping the scales of fairness only to a corrective degree."

It's doubtful that any of his former teachers had shown such compassion to him, but Julian had worked hard and earned excellent grades all on his own merit. Now safely ensconced on the ladder of academic hierarchy, he couldn't be mistreated by meatheads. He had arrived, mostly and to some extent.

Move to Tokyo, the land of littler men? He considered it for a minute after getting out of college. Frankly, he didn't have the balls. Chopsticks and raw fish were one challenge for the conventionally inclined, a non-Latin tongue, yet another. All he had going for him really was his wit, well, better call it, his ability to articulate efficiently, to teach, to verbally transmit information. Trading that out so as not to be noticeably at a loss on a physical plane might not have been a safe bet.

Headley's Elevator Heels, those supposedly hidden lifters of short guys by as much as three whole inches, sat in the box they had arrived in on the highest shelf of the master bedroom walk-in closet. Julian was unlikely to go to the trouble of carting in a stepladder to retrieve them. His original try-on had been enough to convince him that this particular style of shoe would only draw attention to, rather than deflect from his height deficiency. They were idiotic, a huge disappointment. They made him look like he was wearing horse's hooves. And yet, he had declined to return them. Was it to avoid detection or because he was unwilling to give up hope and might one day drag them back out and find that they really did deliver as advertised? He made sure they were sufficiently pushed back on the shelf to avoid the incessant scrutiny of his wife who would undoubtedly mock him; probably even try them on and clomp around the bedroom in them. He could see it now, knowing her as he did.

It's ironic that Julian had considered Amanda to be the best thing that had ever happened to him. He now wondered how he'd gotten it so ass backwards. Amanda turned out to be such a cunt (sorry, but that's the only word for it), but she was a cunt whom he was attached to at the hip by law if no longer by choice. She owned one pair of flats and the tennis sneakers she was wearing when they met. The flats were well worn for the majority of their pre-nuptial relationship. He now counted twenty-seven pairs of high heels. These were the fashion she suddenly favored post marriage. Not the modest one- or two-inch horseshoe shaped heels, but full-on stilettos. She towered over him in them. It was small comfort, but comfort nonetheless that he hadn't been the one to pay for them. She made way more money than he did and, consequently, they kept their finances separate. In fact, she bought her own birthday gifts, and he did his. She spoiled herself. He did not himself, nor could he, prep schoolteachers not being the most lavishly compensated of educators, though it could be argued they should.

The fact that Julian obsessed so relentlessly about his height diminished his efficacy and even likeability as a human being. He had no sense of humor whatsoever. Having been the object of jokes throughout his young life and not unexpectedly finding much the same treatment in the Teacher's Lounge, he wasn't a humor fan in the least. When asked, "Had he heard the one," he rather rudely replied "Yes" before the speaker had even gotten to "about the..." It seemed, at times, he might have been better off in a place where the language was unfamiliar to him, after all.

Barcus was a huge shaggy black lab. Julian was not one for little dogs. He loved Barcus every bit as much as Amanda despised him. And if "despise" is too strong a word, "love" certainly isn't. Amanda liked a spotless home. Julian did too, but not at the expense of his best friend. Dog hair and the occasional slather of stringy drool, muddy paw prints and such were minor sacrifices. Amanda's no-dog-in-the-bed rule was rendered irrelevant when coupled with the newly decreed no-husband-in-the-bed rule and Julian invited Barcus to join him in the guest room down the hall. Everything was on one floor in their suburban ranch house or the two would have relocated to a basement or attic for further separation.

Without question, it was left to Julian to do the walking and feeding and vet visits and subsequent administration of meds when called for. This was fine with him. He was a proud Dad and his four-legged progeny was physically impressive and made him feel like a bigger man somehow. Barcus loved other dogs, was indifferent to cats, liked people, even Amanda, and mostly knew to contain his tremendous affection for Julian so as not to knock him flat on his ass, which happened quite easily when Barcus got over excited.

Fitz, the portly headmaster of the ivory-towered New England school that Julian taught at, had a Pomeranian that he took to work every day. "How pathetic!" Julian thought. As it happened, his opinion of most of his academic colleagues ran along the same critical lines. The chip on his shoulder seemed to make him hyper critical of any perceived human imperfection no matter how hard he had to look to find one. The solitary and notable exception was Lois.

Ms. Lois Coronetti Carson's persona would challenge no stereotypes Ripley's Believe It Or Not! wouldn't stop the presses to squeeze in the explosive novelty of a sturdily built lesbian Physical Education teacher. In a compilation of much more subtle oddities though, her great friendship with little Julian might have made the cut.

They had almost nothing in common, though she did suspect, perhaps wishfully, that he might be gay too. He reacted strongly enough against this theory to render it fertile teasing ground and Lois loved to tease "Juli," as she and very few other people in his life were permitted to call him. He took this surprisingly well. It came down to the fact that he wasn't gay, not even just a little bit. Poking fun at his remarkable shortness was a different story altogether.

"Sometimes I wish that I actually was gay, Lois," he told her more than once. "Women can be so harsh."

"Well. You just be careful what you wish for there, my friend. My life can't exactly be described as gay fabulous or anything. We all have to deal with something."

"…but you gotta' pick yourself up and put on your big boy pants," Julian finished the familiar caution.

They got so close in Lois's first year at 'Fitz Prep' that faculty and students alike thought they were romantically involved with each other, which was weird because they were both also rumored to be gay.

Among the undistinguished students at this below midlevel school, one was the cause of much trouble, one coed by the name of Donna Capucci. She came from Oyster Bay Long Island and was rumored to have eaten large quantities of the town's namesake crustaceans. This, of course, according to all the young boys who couldn't help but get woody around her, was why she was so sexy. Her father was a local big shot who owned a lucrative sand mine and coached the varsity high school football team. Her brothers were on the team and accurately reputed to be entitled blockheads who jumped at any opportunity to go way overboard in defending their baby sister's honor. Her mother wasn't well, and no one ever saw her. She apparently required quite a lot of pharmaceuticals and, it was rightly supposed, Donna could be a resource in this regard for those who sought difficult to come by substances without a prescription. But Donna was no petty drug dealer. She had to be convinced of a legitimate medical need before "prescribing" medications. Her authority on these and many other matters could only be verified by herself as it happened, but this was good enough for all involved. Donna was a passable student too, the total package, though her classmates were convinced that her highly developed bosom was what clinched her respectable grade point average.

Most would assume based on these many assets that she was super popular. Such was not the case. Flat-chested, preppy girls let their envy disguise itself as aversion on strictly moral grounds. The boys were just plain scared of her and the guilty fantasies they cast themselves in with her. This placed Donna in the bottom five least popular. The fact that she couldn't have cared less assured that she'd remain there permanently.

Julian and Lois, being human, were obsessed; all the teachers and administrators were.

"If she wasn't fifteen, I'd have to question whether they were real," Julian said.

"I dreamt about her winning with them. You know, running a hundred-meter dash and edging out a girl who she would have tied with had it not been for those getting her there first," Lois added.

"I didn't know she ran."

"She doesn't. I have her in field hockey and volleyball and really they're more a liability than anything else."

"Hmmm. Well, we can't all excel at everything. She'll be getting an A from me, not for those, of course, or even for any great academic achievement, but just for putting in so much more of an effort than the rest of the nimrods."

"Did you ever play any sports, Juli? If I had to guess, I'd say wrestling."

"Correct, and a little ping pong in college. Oh, and I got kicked out of fencing for being too aggressive."

"No basketball, then?"

"Very funny, ha ha."

Lois liked to half nelson Julian and fake punch him in the belly to emphasize a joke. He didn't mind this as it was done with affection and physical contact is physical contact and he didn't get much at home other than from his dog.

Another of Lois' favorite things was her cocktails and though Julian was not much of a drinker, at least half due to his unmanly lack of capacity, he wasn't opposed to joining her at Mitch's after school to shoot the breeze. His feet didn't reach the footrest, but it was dark enough that no one could really see. The cool thing was that everybody seemed to appear a little taller when they were sitting on a barstool in dim lighting. He liked the sweet and salty nuts too.

"Beer nuts," Lois told him while popping a few in her mouth and munching down with satisfaction.

Their first time there, Julian tried to order a lite beer, but Lois put an end to that.

"Jack on the rocks. Make it two, Mitch."

Mitch was the bartender. Julian always had to watch that he didn't stare too obviously at what looked like a toupee, but he couldn't be quite sure. He asked Lois about it once and she gave him a shrug. That was her answer. Mitch was a nice enough guy. It was rude to stare, but so hard not to, especially after the Jack Daniels started kicking in.

"You drink like a girl. Sippy, Sippy." (Half-nelson, fake belly punch.)

"Well, you drink like a truck driver." (Headshake, pout.) "What do you say, Mitch?"

"Well, between the both of ya, it equals out to like one good customer, and as you can see, I can spare the extra seat at the bar. Except for you're eating me out of beer nuts."

Whenever Julian arrived home from a Lois night, Amanda told him he smelled like alcohol and when he explained he'd just been out with his lesbian friend, she had nothing nice to say about that either. He loved when Amanda worked late. He and Barcus would microwave Lean Cuisines or whatever else was available and plop themselves in front of the TV in the living room. The minute her car beams slung past the bay window though, Julian would turn off the set and make a run for his room. It was exciting, in a funny kind of way. Barcus liked it too.

When Lois asked him why the dual citizenship one day was kind of out of the blue, he told her that it was because he'd been born in Canada.

"Dad, a draft dodger?"

"No, but he was antiwar, that's for sure."

"Guess he made certain you wouldn't have to be dodging any draft."

"What does that mean?"

"Well, buddy, obviously you're too pint-sized to serve."

"Hey, that's hitting below the belt."

"Oh, come on, Juli, I can't even bend down that far." (Shoulder shove.)

"Ok, that's it, I'm done here. I thought you were my friend, Lois, there's a lot of stuff I could say about you. But I don't say it."

"Hey, hey now, calm down, Jul. I am your friend. You know that. Sorry I took it into the size area. I think I'm just having a rough day. Forgive me."

"Geez."

"Besides, I think your shortness makes you way cuter." (Chin chuff.)

The following morning, Julian was in the middle of thinking "If you really only have one friend in the world, you better be ready to forgive them, occasionally getting on your nerves. But Lois knows I hate it when she..." when Donna wafted into his office interrupting his existential ruminations.

Her perfume was something else and she wore a lot of it. Her tits, squeezed snugly into the button-down Peter Pan collar white blouse that on its own would never be mistaken for a sexy article of clothing were considerably more distracting than Mitch's toupee.

"What can I do for you, Donna?"

"Well, it's probably not of the greatest importance, Mr. D, but I just thought that someone should let you know that I'm the only one in our class who is actually reading our assignment, David Copperfield by Charles Dickens."

"I happen to think that that is kind of a big deal, Donna. Like you say, it's the class assignment. How do you suppose your classmates think they're going to get away with not reading the class assignment?"

"Oh, there are plenty of summaries and condensations and things you can get on the internet if you want to. But I can't help it, I just think that's cheating."

"They're cheating themselves as much as anything." (Whip glasses off and wave them in the air professorially.)

"They said they can't get into it because nobody is speaking American. I say what about Harry Potter, they don't speak American either." (Lean in closer, boobs almost resting on desk.)

"Yes, I see your point."

"Anyways, I just thought you should know. Since you are the actual teacher."

Twenty minutes after she left, Julian remained sitting there thinking about her. He wasn't worrying over his other students or David Copperfield or his Lois conundrum or anything other than how he might segue out of his office and down the hall to the men's room without betraying the stick in his pants. He castigated himself most harshly but could smell her perfume just as strongly as if she was still sitting there.

He and Barcus watched the Adult Channel that night. He hoped that there wouldn't be some obvious extra charge affirming the fact on the cable bill. Amanda paid for the cable and had questioned him on individual charges more than once.

"I didn't sign up to pay for your extras," she told him.

He couldn't afford to have a crush on a student, not morally, ethically or any way you looked at it and dearly hoped this incident had been a one off. At the same time, it brought to his attention the fact that he'd been involuntarily celibate for over a year now. As situations go, clearly not a good one.

"You're my favorite teacher," she had said while coyly blowing him a kiss. And it was as if she'd reached under the desk and gently squeezed his balls.

The fact that she had attributed exactly the same distinction to Lois and most likely every other teacher in the school didn't enter his mind. It couldn't have. He had no idea. The time to compare notes would come, but that would be much later.

He was completely clueless.

Things were rapidly devolving with Amanda.

"I can't take this any longer," she had said after they got into it about a certain charge on the cable bill.

"Well then, don't," he replied in a flash of bravado.

"I think you need to divorce me," came out of her mouth and landed like a bomb.

The words alone made both of them jump just a little.

"Why don't you go ahead and divorce me?" Julian asked.

"It's complicated," she said. "As you know I make much more money than you do and I don't think it's fair that you get half of everything I've worked so hard for."

"What?"

"If you divorce me and we sign an agreement to the effect, then we can each just go our separate ways. I'll, of course, allow you to live here until the house sells. If you wish to move right away, I'll understand."

All this time she was thinking to herself "Godammit, why didn't you get a prenup, idiot?" But she had been in love; she thought that's what it was. She wasn't really sure since she had nothing to compare it to. She found that she looked forward to their dates. She liked that he wasn't taller than her and that he didn't insist on children. Love, right? The sex was crazy good, until it wasn't.

"That is very unlikely to be happening, Mrs. Dickerson. You're the one who wants a divorce."

"You're pathetic. What in God's name was I thinking? Am I the only woman who ever found you dateable even for just a brief, unaccountable period of obvious delusion?"

He so wanted to tell her a floridly embellished account of his relationship with Donna, but he didn't dare. Anyway, just because she couldn't see his value didn't mean no other woman could. Would anyone ever say she was their favorite teacher? He thought not. First thing the next day, he'd take this whole matter up with his most trusted advisor, Lois.

"I will not let you let that bitch off the hook, Juli. Not on my watch."

"But what can I do? She wants out and she has a point, it's her money."

"You didn't ask to be put in this position and, remember, she introduced you to a certain lifestyle to which you've grown accustomed. The ranch house should be yours. And for half the price of that Lexus she parades around in, you could have a decent Toyota paid in full. You should have a decent Toyota, Juli, you deserve it."

"You think?"

He knew she was right. Amanda had treated him like a dishrag pretty much from the moment he put a ring on it. He wasn't in love with her anymore so that was good. Still, rejection is rejection even if it's only the final step in a long painful procession toward the bitter end. It made him feel sorry for himself and inevitably caused him to doubt his future prospects. If he had a house and a decent car, though, maybe love would find him again. Amanda didn't know this, but she was right. She had actually been his first ever girlfriend; not a great track record.

If it weren't for Barcus and the fact that he was warned by Lois to not legally abandon his home, he would have preferred to stay away. Instead, he headed home (to the only American ranch in a suburb distinguished for its' ubiquitous Colonial Revival style architecture) each evening after school and more often than ever after bellying up to the bar with Lois who literally did belly up to the bar.

A week or so into the matrimonial standoff, Julian arrived home with the righteous umbrage of the short and slightly drunk. He slammed the door of his Smart Car as much as a Smart Car door could possibly be slammed. He picked up Amanda's Wall Street Journal and tossed it surreptitiously in the neighbor's trash. Amanda had left the divorce paperwork for him to sign on the kitchen table. It vibrated in his hands as if it was radioactive. She wanted a clean split, no sharing of assets. Basically, he was invited to pack a bag and take the dog and that would be that. Part of him wanted to say "yes," not just to avoid confrontation, but also to minimize his own agony. But Lois would not let it go down like that.

He could hear her. "Man up, Juli. I'm not going to let you lie down and play dead while that little whore walks all over you in her spiked heels. Not happening on my watch, my friend. No way, Jose."

He contemplated the good old days. Amanda had surprised him with the new car.

Of course, he was mortified. The smallest possible car for one of the shortest possible grown men, but what could he say? At the time, he really believed she was trying to be nice. He foolishly thought they were on the same side of the net; foolishly! Whatever… It was not helpful to dwell on the past, but a new and less ridiculous vehicle would certainly be a step up.

He took Barcus for a longer than usual walk, though an observer might say that Barcus was walking him. At any event, the whole thing was brisk and both man and dog were ready to tuck into a hearty meal upon their arrival home.

She was there, home early.

"Where's my newspaper?"

"How should I know?"

"Julian, stop playing games. I know you know where my paper is and you know I know it."

"I told you, Amanda, that I don't know where your paper is and if I did know you would be the first to know it."

"Come here, Julian," Amanda said while summoning him over to her desk. She clicked on her laptop, opening a video that, though grainy and fish eyed, did irrefutably show Julian bending down in the driveway and tossing the paper into the neighbor's bin."

"Oh, so you're spying on us now?"

"The camera doesn't lie, Julian. Thank God for modern technology. Now go get it."

Julian sheepishly went out and fetched the paper from the neighbor's garbage. He felt like a dog. He felt worse than a dog. He felt like a very short man being treated like a dog.

"That's better. Don't ever think you can outsmart me, Julian. That would be a grave mistake. Now, what about the paperwork? I assume we're good?"

No, Amanda, no we're not good," Julian raised himself up as far as he could manage and with the gravitas of his maximized stature added, "And I hate that damn car."

Amanda was able to deflect this particular blow and move on to various put-downs and threats and the sad outcome was that Barcus had to settle for plain old kibble and the box of Ritz crackers he shared with his master. That was dinner. But our hero felt great. He had stood up to the bitch for once in his life.

After a beautiful night's sleep, Juli woke up a little hungry, but still feeling like a champ. He toasted up some frozen waffles and cavalierly poured the remainder of the Aunt Jemima over them leaving the empty container for all the world to see. Barcus was happy for a brisk morning constitutional and could not read his master's sudden dismay as they rounded the corner to return home.

Julian broke into a run, which he later wished he hadn't because Barcus responded too enthusiastically to his urgency and dragged him along the ground for thirty yards. He was, for all that, unable to thwart the two guys who apparently had come to repossess his Smart Car.

Lois' Ford Bronco, or her "truck" as she referred to it, was a tall order for Julian, literally. That evening, having sustained various dog dragging injuries to pile on top of the insult of his repossessed vehicle, the climb aboard was that much tougher. In fact, though he tried with all his might, he was mortified to have to surrender and ask for help. Lois lifted him up like an infant, one arm under his legs and the other behind his back and all too handily deposited him on the front seat. Thankfully, it was past dusk and, as they were leaving from Mitch's parking lot, a witness might just assume he had had one too many. Truthfully, as they were leaving from Mitch's, a witness was a highly unlikely thing anyway. The place was that hurting for customers.

"Poor Mitch," Julian managed to think as he reached this point in his analysis.

Thank God for Lois and thank God for a lift 'home.' Not that he could necessarily call it that anymore.

Barcus was clearly innocent of any recollection of that morning's debacle and pleased as ever to receive the unconditional love and unerring loyalty of his best friend Julian. It seemed to him that treats were in order and so they were. What a blessing that Amanda wasn't home and, better yet, a note left in her impeccable script on the kitchen table advised that they wouldn't see her until the weekend.

"Sign the GD paperwork, Julian, you're fucking with the wrong person," read the last sentence in her charming cursive with a heart shaped dot over the "i" in the expletive. It felt as if someone rang a door buzzer installed in the back of his neck, but, happily, the sensation traveling down his spine didn't have far to go and then that was that.

Of the many mouthwatering options offered, Julian and Barcus decided on pizza. The Dominos guy, having been there before, didn't think a tip was so important to wait for if that meant the loss of a pizza touting limb to the jaws of a ravenous beast. He left the pie in its box on the doorstep, ran back to the safety of his car and rang Julian on the phone.

"It's there, Sir."

"'Sir,'" Julian thought. "Nice kid, very polite. 'Sir.' I like that."

Aside from Julian being a bit stiff when it came to their walks, the week was one long delight for the boys. As it turned out, pizza won top dinner choice every night, never mind the expense and Julian was able to leave a generous tip in an envelope taped on to the front door in thanks for the punctual and professional service.

Nothing out of the ordinary occurred at school. Donna asked for another one on one and Julian discreetly managed to evade her knowing the effect she had on him, though involuntary, was inappropriate in the extreme. A class trip to the nation's capital was planned for the following weekend and that sucked up what little could be found of his students' attention spans even on a good day.

Julian dreaded the return of his soon to be ex-wife and anticipated two long days and nights of browbeating, for which he worried he may not be a match. Lois propped him up as best she could, even Mitch weighed in.

"Don't sign nothin', Julian. Listen to your friend Lois here," Mitch wagged gnarly forefinger in Julian's face.

"Mitch, I told you, you should have bought a house with a foundation, like a real house," Lois elbowed Julian in the ribs as she continued. "His home with Doreen was mobile, mobile as in, on wheels mobile."

"Lois always said to me, 'Get a house that's stuck to the ground, Mitch. You can't feel settled and secure if you live in a house that could roll down a hill or something.' This is why I'm telling you, Julian, listen to her," he nodded to Lois as he finished drying off a beer mug and placed it beside its brothers on the shelf.

"That's right, I warned him, but I can't claim to have known that Doreen was gonna get herself a low-life new boyfriend with a truck and a trailer hitch."

"So when did you build the house out back? After she left?"

"No, I had started it before she left, but it was taking too long I guess and Doreen, she's a restless one. If business had been better, I could have finished the place and we would have had a real nice home back there."

"You're living there now, aren't you?"

"Yup, but it still has a ways to go. I have to run here to use the facilities and the outdoor shower is only good while it's warm out. Someday, I'll get it done and maybe Doreen will come on back home. But I haven't been able to track her down yet."

"Why, in God's name would you even want to track her down? Look what she left you with, Mitch, tell Julian what she left you with."

"Well, I went home to the trailer that night and all that was left was an empty propane tank."

"You deserve more than a propane tank with what you've put up with Juli. Don't let that bitch do to you what Doreen did to Mitch, bless his soul."

"That's right, don't go trusting no women. Ahh, except for Lois who is not really a woman, or I mean, in that same kind of way."

"Mitch, you wanna buy me a drink, I'll take that remark as a compliment."

"Deal."

CHAPTER Two

Donna's note read:

Dear Professor Dickerson,

It is with all do respect for which I write this to you today. I have recently pointed out that a bunch or almost all my fellow students who among us attend your English Literature class have been assigned to reading certain materials that you have told us to read. This being said and as I complained in our last meeting, they are still not reading it. It has come to my attention that you have not said anything to our class about this or maybe I am just ignorant of any such admonition. I again point your awareness to the following:

A. I don't want to be the only student doing the actual reading.

B. I do not really regard this as having a beneficial resultation on the class as a whole.

C. I will be happy to meet you on this important subject if you think it will help and don't want to make me feel like you are avoiding me about this.

Sincerely yours,

Donna (Your best Student Wink Wink)

J ulian had to adjust his eyes multiple times through the reading of Donna's latest heartfelt missive. Too many shots, not enough sleep. He was going to have to cut back on the indulgent lifestyle Lois seemed to thrive on. She regularly outdrank him, at least three to one and always turned up fresh as a daisy each morning, spreading good cheer and morally questionable jokes in the Teacher's Lounge.

When Julian suggested a movie night, just to change the pace, she replied. "I got over a hundred channels of TV for which I pay a monthly fortune."

"I thought you said you spliced into your neighbor's cable."

"What's the difference? My neighbor shells out a pile of cash and I would too if I didn't have the brains God gave me."

"Movies are cheaper than Mitch's."

"Yeah, but Mitch's has free beer nuts. The movies don't have free beer nuts and you buy a large popcorn, you could put a down payment on a condo for less."

"I do love the nuts, Lois but that doesn't mean I like feeling hungover every other day."

"You're a novice, Juli. Don't worry, you'll get the hang of it. The trick is to keep getting back on the horse."

Julian knew when to exit a debate with Lois; usually after about the third or fourth volley, or risk her spiking the ball on your head. At the end of the day, he preferred having a friend and a hangover than a head full of clarity with which to contemplate having not a friend in the world.

As he was reading Donna's note for the second time, Lois barged in and plopped down in the guest chair. Even though Julian's desk was not superimposing, and his adjustable office chair was maxed out to its highest setting, the image of him still brought to mind bring-your-child-to-work day. Lois didn't say this even though she thought it… every time.

"Who's that from? Your secret admirer?" Lois reached for the note and snapped her fingers to emphasize she meant business. Julian handed it over.

"My God, this kid is persistent. Why don't you just get it over with and meet with her, Jules?"

"Not comfortable doing that, Lois. Not right at the moment anyway."

"What are you, your own thought police? You're not acting on it, Juli; it's not some big sin to think something."

"That's the thing, I don't trust myself; not with her being so goddamn flirtatious and all."

"Three things; you could send her a note, address the issue with the class as a whole or have a meeting with me here too, which I'd be more than happy to do for you."

"Most of the class hates me as is. If I make a big deal of this, it will only make matters worse. Plus, I need to pass a few of them or I'm putting my own job at risk and if I force them to read the actual material instead of a summary thereof, they either will do so and won't get it or they won't do so and won't get it and then I have to fail all of them. For God sake, Donna, who actually did read it, didn't do as well on a pop quiz I gave recently as the Cliff note kids did."

"What about a note?"

"I am not in favor of documentation. It can come back to bite you."

"Okay, then, set up the meeting, I'll be here. I got your back, Juli."

"Thanks, Lois. Thanks."

"Now come on, let's blow this popsicle stand. I took the liberty of reserving the two best barstools in the house at Mitch's. We don't want to be late."

That one extra shot of tequila had somehow counteracted the effect of the previous five. Maybe too, the stand-your-ground in the divorce pep talk from his two closest friends and confidantes had propped Julian back up again. This surge of confidence would have been quite bracing had his first step inside the house not produced an audible squish and a familiar unpleasant odor. Barcus had waited just as long as Barcus could. He skulked over to his master fully aware that there may be consequences for his lack of control.

"Never mind," Julian conveyed with a big smile and a doggy pat on the head. "Never mind, boy, who's a good boy?"

It was entirely his fault, he thought, and so began the self-castigation that, mixed with the excess of alcohol, brought Julian stumbling back into a slurry, shoulder drooping puddle of regret.

"What the hell, Julian, what the hell?" he murmured as he cleaned up the pile of shit and tried not to get overly metaphorical.

It was to be their last night together before Amanda's woeful homecoming. By some dumb and unwelcome luck, the familiar hum of the Lexus was just preceded by a sweep of headlight beams through the bay window and across the living room wall. The front door swung open, and Amanda looked, sneered, threw her keys down on the kitchen table, mock laughed and retired to her room.

"Just like a piece of shit," Julian announced to his tail wagging partner. "That's how she treats me and I'm sick of it."

During the course of a very long walk around the neighborhood at eleven something at night, Julian considered whether it was too late to dial up Lois and share this latest transgression on the part of his erstwhile one true love. He knew his friend well enough to surmise she'd be in a deep sleep, but felt so rotten, so low that his urge was meth-head intense, and he went for it.

"You gotta be kidding me, calling at this hour, Juli."

"But you're up, aren't you?"

"I'm up, but it's not like it isn't way past my bedtime. You don't get gorgeous like this gorgeous without your beauty rest, my friend. And what are you doing wandering the streets after dark. This is not good for your health and stability, Jul."

"She's back. Came home early and found me cleaning up after poor Barcus who couldn't hold it in because Daddy was out carousing again. She was abusive without even having to say a word, not a word, Lois."

"Like I'm telling you now for like the entire time I've known you, you've got to stand up for yourself, little man. Tiny, but mighty, like they say, sticks and stones and words or no words, Jul. But, listen, you're not the only one with problems. You could maybe just once ask what I'm doing up at this hour."

"First of all please, don't call me 'tiny,' I hate when you call me 'tiny' and you know that."

"Fine, I won't call you that, now ask me."

"Ask you what?"

"Why I'm awake, Julian, why I'm awake still."

"Okay, why are you?"

"Why am I what?"

"Geez, Lois, why are you awake?"

"I'm awake because I'm upset and I can't sleep. And what I'm upset about is my daughter. She can't find a date for her Senior Prom and her father tells me she is showing all the signs of slipping into one of her sessions. Now I know she's not the same as other girls, but at least she took after her father in the looks department. She's got that going for her."

"Hey, Lo, don't be so hard on yourself and what do you mean she's not like other girls."

"She's a little bit of a head case, Jules; depression and all that and not just depression, debilitating depression like skipping school for a month, sometimes as much as a year, at a time, can't get out of bed depression. They call it atypical for lack of any better label, but even her atypical is atypical. Makes you feel helpless."

"God, I'm really sorry, I had no idea, how come you never mentioned this?"

"I don't like to talk about it. But, whatever, it doesn't mean she doesn't have dreams of a magical prom night like every other kid. This will be her second one."

"Wait, what do you mean her second one?"

"She had to repeat senior year. She's had to repeat a bunch of years due to not being able to get out of bed and go to school. She's three years older than her classmates so of course it's hard to find a date. It just breaks my heart. So, yeah, I can't sleep, I'm worried about my Shelley."

"I'm so sorry, Lois. Maybe she would have been better off staying with you after the split. Maybe you could have protected her better, steered her clear of all this."

"Like I told you, Jul, I wasn't in a very happy place at the time. Her father is a great guy and he and his mother have done as good a job with the kid as anyone could. Better than me, I think, probably way better."

"Lois, you always tell me not to put myself down so now I'm going to tell that to you. I've got your back. Anything I can do to help, I mean anything, you just let me know. And, if it's any consolation to you, I also missed my prom."

"Thanks, little buddy. You're a keeper. Now let's both try to get some sleep. Tomorrow is a new day."

Julian, who rarely experienced propping someone else up or being sought out for comfort and advice, felt pretty good about himself by the time he and Barcus tiptoed down the hallway to their man cave. He was soon to wrap his arms around his great warm beast of a man's best friend and fall into a deep and restoring slumber. This respite may not have been as easily attained if he had known what his friend Lois was busy cooking up and that he soon would be implored, given his youthful appearance, to act as her daughter Shelley's prom date.

Julian woke up with both a physical and emotional hangover despite the support of one best friend and the warm comfort of the other. He wondered at Barcus' enthusiasm for life and contemplated the great variety of dog breeds and sizes. He guessed he himself would have been a teacup; prized for his diminutiveness. How great would that have been. How cool would it be if people were less elitist about size. He heard Amanda's high heels clicking down the hallway and soon smelled the aroma of Hazelnut flavored coffee. He hated Hazelnut flavored coffee and would routinely wait until she was gone, dump almost a whole pot of the stuff down the sink and start from scratch. They had nothing in common, nothing. Granted, she, too, was petite and only had a couple of inches on him, but that was in bare feet and she never ever was in feet with less than a three inch lift. Even her flip flops had several extra layers of rubber sole "platforms."

And here again came the click, click, click down the hallway, except this time it was coming toward him and Barcus. He instinctively jumped back into bed and pulled the covers over himself despite the fact that he was now fully dressed. The door swung open and she stood there holding the doorknob and staring, glaring really.

"If you don't sign the papers this week, this week, Julian, you are going to regret it. The gloves will be coming off and you and Chewbacca will be out on the street. I'm done fooling around here. I've been as reasonable as I can be. The nice me is getting very impatient, and I'm sure you're aware that the not so nice me is somebody you do not want to tangle with. Look at you, a grown man in bed with your doggie and it's almost 8 a.m., some work ethic. Thank god we didn't have any children to see their father behaving like this."

With that and before Julian could muster a word in defense or retaliation, she slammed the door and clicked, clicked, clicked back down the hallway and out the front door.

Un-hazelnut coffee, instant oatmeal and a brisk walk with Barcus helped to restore Julian's nerves. Lois pulled up in her truck and gave a long, loud honk.

Julian swung himself up into the passenger seat with some effort and a gratifying sense of accomplishment. Lois, who was uncharacteristically grumpy, made a comment about a child seat that Julian let graze off him; he was in no condition to push back and he needed the ride and he needed his friend.

Sacred Heart of Jesus Concord Jesuit Preparatory Academy sat on a mountain top from which such sweeping vistas of the lush and majestic Hudson Valley presented themselves that an onlooker could barely take it all in. At times, it made Julian feel like the master of the universe, towering over the vast kingdom fanning out for eternity all about their lord and conqueror. This reverie was often undone by the time he had climbed the granite steps to the main building and had to contend with the carved wooden, ungodly heavy entrance doors whose brass knob was at just such a height as to give him scant leverage against opening the damn things. It was best if someone else happened to be coming or going or if Lois had to stop there first before heading down to the recreation center.

It was just his luck that, on this particular occasion, Lois had a meeting scheduled with Purchasing to see about acquiring a new volleyball net. The existing equipment was full of holes chewed by rodents who were ubiquitous and uncontrollable in this neck of the woods. These holes had caused all kinds of disputes on the field of play with one side swearing the ball had sailed over the net while the other side insisting that it had clearly passed through a giant breach. Lois had had enough of this. It was time for a new net. Of course, Julian wholeheartedly supported her in this matter.

"Even if I wasn't friends with you, Lois, I couldn't argue against your side of the issue. So what if it'll be the second net in three months? You didn't invite the mice to nest in your equipment room. There's nothing you could have done."

Such was the pep talk Julian was giving Lois when Headmaster "Fitz" Sebastian Fitzgerald IV, entered the faculty lounge. His Pomeranian "Dahlila" was, as usual, in tow. Her tongue lolled out of her mouth and her eyes looked like they were about to pop out of her face. In greeting, she bared her raggedy teeth and growled under her breath as if her Dad wouldn't hear her, but the lowly help would get the message loud and clear.

"Well, a very good morning to you two. Up to no good, I suspect," Fitz said in his accustomed jovial yet random style.

"Plotting to take over the school, is it? Kick the old fellow to the curb? Turn the institution into a revolutionary stronghold and seize control of the surrounding hamlets, are we? Heh?"

He laughed and elbowed Julian in the arm causing his coffee to spill and his khaki pants to be embarrassingly splattered about the crotch.

Fitz hastily grabbed a paper napkin and began dabbing at Julian's lap causing a most unseemly reaction and necessitating Julian bolting for the men's room. Lois would not like being left alone with Fitz and company, but Julian would explain later. Much water and soap produced little good result. Julian determined it would need be a sweater around the waist and stay seated behind his desk and not get up to use the blackboard day.

As he returned to the lounge, he was too late to prevent Lois attempting to pet Dahlia who instantly inflicted the second catastrophe of their encounter with Fitz. Fitz quite mildly reprimanded his precious pet after expressing mock shock at the aberration of her unfriendliness while Lois wrapped her hand in a napkin and waved off Fitz's assurances that Dahlila had all her shots.

It was Lois's turn to excuse herself from the table and so she did. Fitz took this opportunity to pal up to Julian and get personal.

"So, is it true? You can confide in me, Julian. I wouldn't be Headmaster if I was one to spill secrets and tell tales, you know."

"Is what true, Sir? (Julian knew Fitz loved it when people called him "Sir")

"Oh my, no need for the honorific, young man." (Julian took note that he and Fitz were right about the same age.) "But I do appreciate the sign of respect, there is far too little of it in contemporary orthodoxy. But do tell me, is your Lois a hot potato in the sack, is that the attraction? Just between us gentlemen, you understand."

"I honestly don't know what you're getting at. Forgive me, but you think that Lois and I are a couple? Really? Really, Sir?"

"Well come on, Boy. Everybody knows. They say you two lovebirds sneak off to Mitch's almost daily after work."

"I'm married, or at least for a little while longer."

"Wrecked the marriage, has it?"

"No, no, the marriage was already wrecked. It's just, Lois and I are the best of friends, period end of sentence… Sir."

Julian felt that he was failing to convince Fitz and that the Head of School definitely preferred his own version of the details of Julian's personal life. "Where the hell is Lois?" he wondered and then quickly considered that her return might not be purely advantageous under the circumstances. But return she did, at just such a point where Fitz, and by default Julian, had to pretend they weren't discussing anything having to do with her.

"Yes, I agree that Shakespeare might be a bit aggressive right now, but let's not give up entirely, Mr. Dickerson. What say?"

"Point well taken, Sir"

"What did I miss?" Lois asked with a tinge of ironic assumption that only Julian detected.

"Nothing, my dear, nothing at all. Just some wonky academic hoopla; you have relieved us indeed, saved us from our own tedious selves."

It was not a very busy morning for the Faculty Lounge. It was early. The few people who did trudge in carried steaming to-go cups despite the free coffee, fresh by an hour or two and kept tepid on its own heating element. It was this brew that Julian had come to rely on as Lois was not one to stop at Starbucks, 'a rip-off,' and because his thermos had been repossessed with his Smart Car.

There was some prestige to be garnered in being seen with Fitz at the table. Julian tried not to preen as his colleagues trickled in and each ran his or her own surreptitious reconnaissance.

All heads turned when pretty, tight ass, posture conscientious Sharon, Fitz's trusted assistant marched through the door.

"Dr. Fitzgerald, Sir, I beg your pardon for the interruption, but there is a matter of some urgency that requires your immediate attention."

"Well, duty calls me away from the pleasantries afforded by a rich exchange with two of the valued colleagues it's my privilege to have in my employ. Somebody's gotta do it, hey? Bon chance, Dickerson and dear Lois, the pleasure was all mine. Good day then, the Head of School never sleeps as they say."

Julian stood up and stretched out his hand for a shake but withdrew it when Dahlila bared her little needle teeth.

"Good day, Sir."

"Yeah, have a good one, Boss."

Sharon waited for Fitzgerald to get up, Dahlila in tow and held the door open for them. As she did so, she casted one last look around the room choosing to settle just briefly on Julian, lower her glance to his crotch area and wag her head in the universal appraisal that said "Loser, loser, loser you pathetic little, loser." Julian flushed, looked down at his stained trousers and realized that this was going to be a really shitty day. He grabbed his sweater, tied it around his waist, took one more cup of "I can't believe it's coffee" and wished his pal Lois good luck on her big meeting with the finance office. Julian's classroom was yet empty, but for one Donna Cappucci pretending to be way too absorbed in learning to notice her teacher's arrival. He too proceeded to pretend not to notice her until she could no longer bear it and interrupted the silence trying to sound nonchalant.

"Oh, hey there, Mr. D. I finally have you by myself. Did you get my multitude of messages that I sent to you? Because if you did, I'm starting to have the idea that I've made you not pleased in some comprehensive-less way. I'm trying my best here, Mr. D, but how can I do my best if my own teacher is not teaching to me, or avoids my reaching outs as if I no longer exist? How about it?"

"Please, Donna, it's okay. Please don't take it personally. My life has been a bit more complicated lately. I'm awfully sorry I haven't gotten around to responding to you. Really I am."

"Don't worry about me starting to feel a little like Dora the child wife out of Dickens's David Copperfield, which we're studying or at least I am studying considering the rest of the class really isn't. But enough about me, now all of my concern is suddenly directed in the direction of you."

"That's kind of you, Donna, and I do appreciate it, but my problems have been personal and of the adult variety. I would never presume to burden a child with my misfortune."

Julian thought briefly about this last statement, reflecting how he was mirroring Donna's earnest and overwrought manner of expression.

"What an idiot I am," he thought.

"Well, Mr. D, if you can't think of me as a confidante of the most trustable variety, then at least please don't think of me as a child. It's making me feel like Dora from Charles Dickens's David Copperfield all over again. I have seen a lot of things even if I'm not so old. That I can tell you."

Not trusting himself to respond at length, Julian just said, "I hear you, Donna. Yes, you are a mature young lady, yes, you certainly are."

"Thank you. I was tempted to go to the administration to protest your unresponsiveness, but believe me, I could not do it and I won't, unless against my will. I have no choice. If you would like to discuss adult matters, I will gladly participate in such a conversation. Meanwhile, there is still the problem of our entire class cheating on the great Charles Dickens just because he speaks more refined than they do or ever will if they don't even try."

"You make an excellent point, and I will bring it up during today's class. Good work, Capucci."

"Oh dear, Sir, we might be having a meeting of the minds, but you need not call me Cappucci. Call me Donna, you always call me Donna."

"Sure thing."

"Sure thing, who?"

"Donna, alright? Sure thing, Donna."

When raised before the class, the subject of short cutting derived a good deal of foot shuffling and chair leg scraping and little else. Donna, of course, raised her hand to weigh in, but Julian had cleverly timed the admonition for the end of the period and was therefore saved by the bell. In the primal din that followed the break of every class and slipping unnoticed through the disorganized herd, Julian made his escape. He was convinced that his stern warning would gain two things, a lot of chair scraping and the temporary removal of Donna off his back.

At lunchtime, Julian took the hot pocket he had microwaved at the lounge and a bottle of Pepsi and walked down toward the recreation building. He found Lois on the phone in her office. She nodded toward him and waved him to have a seat on the bleacher bench in front of her desk.

"Yeah, yeah, of course it's a regulation NCAA net, we're not using it for Badminton over here. You don't, huh? Well, somebody has to repair these things. What do people do when they need a net repair? Just tell me who I can call about this. I'm not about to buy a brand-new net when the one I have is perfectly good except for a few holes. Oh yeah, well that just isn't very helpful at all now, is it? I'll be sure to remember this when I'm in the market for a new net. You can bet I will never, ever buy from you again. Not on your life."

Lois banged the phone down with such force that Julian thought she might need to shop for a repairer of those too.

"Lemme guess, they said no to the new net."

"Fuckin tightwads. I'll tell you, Juli, they got no appreciation for athletics. Art supplies, fucking art supplies. 'Who do I make out the check to, Mrs. Darlington?' But a piece of athletic equipment where people will actually learn something about hand eye coordination and not being a sore loser. No, not important enough, not nearly as important as some piece of shit squiggles on a fancyass piece of shit million-dollar friggin piece of friggin papyrus or some shit. Why do I put up with this? If I wasn't that close to retirement, my friend, you know what I would do?"

"What, Lois, what would you do?"

"I'd start a friggin volleyball net repair business, be my own boss. Take in tennis nets and hockey and soccer goals, do it all, Jul."

"If you do, you're taking me with you, Lois."

"You could run the front office. We could even open a division for custom nets for youngsters and small people. You could be in charge of that."

"Very funny, Lois. Ha ha."

"Oh c'mon, Jul, I was just pulling your leg. Can't you see I'm having a rough day?"

"Look, Lois. You leave here, I leave here, alright? But enough with the short person jokes. You know how I feel about short person jokes, alright?"

Lois opened the mini fridge behind her desk and popped the tab on a cold can of Schlitz.

"I'll drink to that, my friend."

Julian instinctively glanced at the door ready to oppose any potential interloper. "Lois, put that away."

"Don't be such a chicken shit, Jul. I reserve this for special occasions. Anyway, what are they going to do, fire me? So, we'll just start that business of ours a little sooner if they fire me. What d'you say, Buddy? Can I offer you a cold one?"

After one last scan of the periphery, Julian succumbed to the temptation of one for the road. And before he knew it the one was no longer a can but a six-pack. The reverie and laughs and giddy feeling of being a little kid getting away with a forbidden smoke on the municipal tennis court gave way to the terrifying wakeup call of his buzzing phone. To make matters worse, it was Headmaster Fitz.

"Yes, Sir. At your service, Sir," Julian enunciated as best he could.

"You need to see me? Right now? It can't wait until the morning? Okay, okay, I'm a little ways away from the administrative building just at the moment."

"Yes, yes, sir. No problem. You bet. Rightio, Sir. Whatever you need." Julian tapped off the call and put his head in his hands.

"That was Fitz, I am summoned. He's going to know I've been drinking, Lois. What the hell are we going to do? This could be the end. This could be the end and it could be the worst week of my life so far. Donna, that little shit. Donna obviously wasn't satisfied that I've taken her seriously enough."

"Seriously about what, Jul?"

"About the other kids in the class using shortcuts and not actually reading their assignment."

"You mean like Cliff Notes?"

"Yes, like that."

Lois swiveled around in the faux walnut and vinyl executive chair of which she was quite proud and pointed to the framed degree hanging on the wall behind her. She tapped on the glass with her handy field hockey stick.

"See this, Jule? Well, this, you would not be seeing if it wasn't for Cliff Notes. No Cliff Notes, no degree, capice? Even back in my day most kids hated reading whole, entire books and now, nowadays? Forget about it."

"Thank you for your insight. That's just great to know for an English Literature teacher. But hey, I'm not their school counselor. You can lead a horse to water and all. I think Dickens is just, sadly, not relatable enough anymore. Maybe it's too advanced."

"Here, drink this."

Lois slid a large yellow green bottle of Gatorade across her desk and watched approvingly as Julian glugged it down.

"Feel better?"

"Better."

"Now go get 'em, Tiger. Don't even worry about it. It's past two o'clock, Fitz will be so deep into his own cups he won't even notice that you can't walk a straight line and you smell like a brewery; a micro-brewery, hee-hee!"

"Very not funny, Lois."

"Oh, c'mon little guy. Embrace your adorableness, just embrace it."

Julian sighed and shook his head and almost lost his balance getting up from the bleacher bench. Lois took him through a brief jumping jack routine to get the blood recirculating and off he went with trepidation cloaking him like a prayer shawl in the direction of the doors he always had an embarrassingly difficult time opening.

The meeting with the Head of School was not nearly the dreadful affair he had imagined. There was no mention of Donna, only further light banter and ridiculous innuendo with reference to his supposed affair with Lois. Fitz clearly relished this scenario and nothing Julian said could convince him that Lois was not, in fact, his lover. Fitz assumed that Julian was being coy or defensive or both, but the winks he continued to cast Julian's way seemed to affirm a secret understanding between the two men that words could not divert or diffuse.

Julian began to worry that he'd miss his ride home with Lois if they didn't wrap this odd conversation up and started to believe that the only reason Fitz summoned him was to dish about his imagined love life. But when Fitz pronounced "but the real reason I called you here…" Julian's original terror returned, and he braced himself for the upbraiding that was about to come. He glanced at Dahlila, who defended her father's prodigious belly and bared her teeth at Julian as if to warn that she could eat him for lunch.

"As you may be aware, young man, and particularly in light of your chosen field of romantic literature, you know very well how potent is the hand of fate. No?"

"Yes, Sir. Very potent, Sir."

"Well, then, it shouldn't surprise you all that much when I tell you that the reason I was pulled away from our lovely tete a tete this morning was that Les Parker had taken ill and Colleen and he had to cancel as chaperones for the class trip this weekend. At first, I was in a tizzy and then, I thought, Hah! Divine inspiration, Julian and Lois; Julian and Lois. It was meant to be!"

"Forgive me, Sir, but what, what was meant to be?"

"Hold onto your seat, Boy. You and Lois are going to our nation's capital for a weekend of kid corralling that may just avail you a precious moment or two of adult privacy. No, am I right?"

Mitch could see that Lois was in no mood for chitchat. He poured her a beer and made certain it didn't have more than half an inch of head. With a nod, Lois conveyed to Mitch she'd be having a bourbon chaser too. He translated her glance in Julian's direction as meaning "You can give him the same." and so he did.

Lois downed both bourbon and beer in short order and banged each empty glass so hard on the bar that she put another couple of dents in the well-worn maple. Mitch instinctively ran a wet bar rag over the surface and quickly supplied the refills he knew would be expected to appear at speed. As Lois downed those, he prepared round three, even going so far as to sacrifice the second flight of clean glassware. Julian munched on beer nuts and sipped his drinks relatively timidly. Lois normally would have chided him for this, but she was in so rotten a mood that even teasing her little buddy had lost its appeal.

Mitch changed the channel on his TV, his favorite soap notwithstanding. He was thinking maybe the ballgame could lift his best customer and friend out of her funk.

"Turn that thing down, Mitch. Can't you see I'm trying to think here?" Lois said.

"Sorry, Doll. I just thought…"

"Well, don't think, Mitch, okay? Thinking is not a good look for you."

"Hey, hey, Lois c'mon now," Julian bravely offered in Mitch's defense.

"You, you have nothing to say on the subject, little man. You're the one who got us into this pickle in the first place, as if my day wasn't going bad enough, you go and volunteer us to chaperone a bunch of snot nosed brats on a bus trip to see the friggin Washington Monument and sniff cherry blossoms."

"It's not my fault, Lois. I so did not volunteer us. It was all Fitz. He was in a bind."

"Fitz was in a bind, my ass. And now everyone is going to think we're an item. You and me are an item, Julian? God!"

Mitch shoved Lois's refills across the bar, picked up Julian's shot glass and saw that he wasn't quite done and set it back down as gingerly as possible so as not to trigger scrutiny.

It wasn't the first time Julian noted that Mitch had his back and he made a mental calculation that doubled the tip he'd be leaving this evening. Well, or at least 25% above the usual. Meanwhile, he thought it might be a good idea to fill Mitch in and hoped that in doing so he could indirectly and perhaps more effectively lay out his case for Lois's consideration.

"These kids, Mitch. These school kids can be awfully tricky. I can tell you, Buddy. I've seen it all. Lois has seen it all. Both of us, both of us have to deal with it every day. The trickiness. Well, there's this one girl, quite voluptuous as it happens, and the kind of girl who could get someone into real trouble and she has been on my case in a very demanding way, but also flirtatiously and when I tell you it's confusing, oh boy, is it confusing. Lois can back me up on this. Can't you, Lois."

"Whatever, Julian. I don't even know where the hell you think you're going with this. Do you know where you're going with this?"

"Yes, Lois, as a matter of fact I do." Julian adjusted himself that half inch taller that was all the inch available to him. "As it happens, Mitch, just this morning, this girl threatened to cause trouble for me with the school administration. Not only that, but Lois here had experienced a bit of a setback and proposed some retaliatory beers in her office during school hours, which I believe you are aware is against the rules. So, when Fitz, the head guy, summoned me to his office, I had reason to believe it was curtains. I was a dead man walking, a goner, toast, no…"

"Alright already, we get the picture. Where exactly are you taking us, Julian? Another one of your merry go round rides?"

"I'm trying to describe my mindset, Lois. You're the one who's always talking about how important mindsets are so I'm telling you what mine was at the time, this afternoon when our dear Head of School suddenly invited me to come to his office, which you know never happens. So, Mitch, it was a great relief when Fitz said to me he wanted Lois and me to fill in as chaperones for the school trip this coming weekend. Was I going to say no? Under those circumstances, and considering that particular mindset, was I about to turn the guy down? No, I don't think so."

"What he didn't think, Mitch. What my friend here didn't think is that I might not want to be dragged into this whole mess right along with him because his mindset made him sign me up for a weekend in hell with a busload of juvenile delinquents traipsing around Washington D. fucking C. in the heat holding up a little white flag in hopes that they stick with the group and we don't have to call in the Secret Service and the National Guard."

"Maybe it won't be so bad, Lois. You probably get to stay in a motel. You love motels."

"Are we staying in a motel, Jul?"

"Best Western."

"I do like Best Western. It's a decent chain. Okay, I tell you what, after you called me up in the middle of the night and I was all worried about Shelly, my kid, not having a date for Prom and you said you'd do anything for me, I got a great idea. You can be Shelley's date."

"Wait, what?"

"She's a high school kid, right?" Mitch asked.

"That's right, but my Shelley is older than her classmates since she got held back a couple of times and Julian could pass for around her age."

"Oh no, my friend, you cannot be serious. You're asking me to go to a High School Prom and pretend to be someone I'm not? No way!"

Julian was adamant, but his will was no match for Lois's go-to no-carrot-all-stick method of persuasion. Basically, if he didn't take her daughter to the prom, she would call in sick for the trip to D.C.

"God, you are too much, Lois. Geez, me going to a friggin prom."

"The good news is that you've been pre-approved by your prom date. I sent Shelley your picture, She thinks you're cute. Go figure, Jules."

"Very funny."

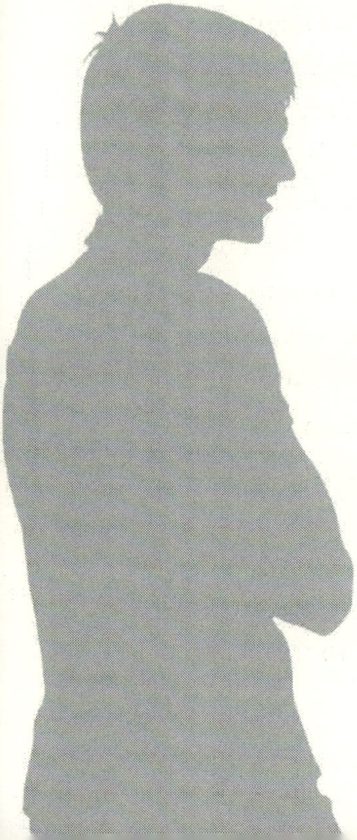

CHAPTER
Three

As Lois and Julian were assembling at the main entrance to the school, Mitch was relocating the last of the bowls of nuts from the bar where Barcus would no longer be able to reach them. "Like father, like son," he thought and then wondered seriously what he had gotten himself into.

The chaperones were bleary eyed at this ungodly hour and Lois found this good reason to be newly steamed with her little friend. The one blessing was that they found their wards far more subdued than usual. As the young zombies shuffled onto the bus one by one, they appeared resigned to an unhappy yet inevitable fate. Only Donna exhibited perkiness, as was her custom. She made certain to commandeer a seat just behind Julian and Lois who sat in the front row flanking the driver.

Tirana eased the big bus down the long and splendid drive beneath a canopy of fresh green maple leaves. The sun twinkled through the giant windshield until they pulled onto 95 and met with the blinding glare of the naked highway. Julian could see why the driver sported something akin to tinted shop goggles without the elastic strap. Tirana was actually not bad looking, he thought, and wondered whether she was in fact as diminutive as she appeared in the big bus seat below. She operated her vehicle with impressive finesse. A cool character, he thought, with admiration and a bit of trepidation.

Lois broke the ice, surprisingly, considering her foul mood.

"Been down the road a few miles or so I can see," she said to Tirana, her voice raised over the boastful grinding of the power tram.

"You don't even know, Girl. I figure I spent more time in this seat than any other seat ever."

"Even the toilet?" Julian asked, thinking he was being funny.

Lois nudged him hard and Tirana just raised her eyebrows over the top of her utilitarian eyewear and shook her head as if to say "So not funny, little man." Nobody talked for the next hundred miles, except, of course, for Donna, who wanted to know from Julian that he thought her recent book report superior to those of her regrettable classmates. Seeing that Lois was making an effort to doze off, Julian uncharacteristically shushed her and mimed the word "later" as best he could multiple times until Donna seemed to agree to understand what he was mouthing to her.

They finally pulled into a busy rest area and Julian sought to make amends with Tirana by offering to get her a coffee.

"Light and sweet. I think there's a Dunkin's here. If not, I'll take a coke. Don't bring me any of that Starbucks crap, please."

"Got it. Lois?"

"I'll take the same, Julian, anything but that crap from Starbucks. I'm so with you on that, Tirana."

Still in zombie mode, the youngsters stumbled down the aisle. The three adults emphasized the need for them to hurry it up and forecasted a departure in exactly ten minutes.

Half an hour later, Julian was delivering a second round of coffees and sugar donuts to Lois and Tirana who seemed less phased by the delay as they clearly found one another's company distracting. Julian was dispatched to go corral the students and get them the hell back on the bus.

"I haven't even had time to finish my first cup of coffee" was his best defense, but it fell on deaf ears and off he went. Always the good guy, chivalrous to a fault, he fetched the brats while Lois and Tirana enjoyed their tete a tete.

Julian found his mission to be nearly impossible and began to realize what the ensuing 48 hours would look like. After escorting small groups of freshly amped up teenagers back to the parking lot, he realized he'd never be able to finish the job alone. He engaged a friendly Security Guard who obviously had dealt with this sort of thing before. The guard sent Julian to "Headquarters" to broadcast an appeal over the PA system and walkie talkied his colleagues to retrieve anyone in the place below the age of sixteen. As Julian headed back to the front entrance, one such security guard stopped him and questioned him, apparently assuming that Julian was one of the kids. This did not sit well.

A little cloud hung over Julian and followed him into the bus, which now seemed bursting with unwelcome energy.

Indiscriminate shouting, laughing, and screaming was audible graffiti defiling the peace. Julian looked to Lois for emotional support and solidarity in disapproval, but Lois was beaming. Julian had never seen her so happy. Not one to be fooled, he quickly assessed that Lois and Tirana were actively making some kind of love connection at a velocity common only to women of their particular sexual persuasion. (Though you could have fooled him about Tirana.) When Lois had told him her favorite joke—"What does a lesbian bring on a second date?...A U-Haul"—he hadn't realized how true to life this would prove to be.

He was alone in his misery. Once again, he'd been mistaken for a child and now his best friend was off to the races with the only other adult in the vicinity. He borrowed Lois earbuds and buried himself in the plaintive righteousness of The Indigo Girls. It beat hearing those kids and having been exposed so many times during rides home with Lois, he even knew many of the words. To his surprise and qualified relief, he found that he could really get into Lois favorite lesbian singing duo. He was careful not to let any actual sound escape his lips. Nobody needed to hear him singing along to "Beauty Queen Sister."

Tirana was clearly showing off for her new 'friend.' The bus pulled into the Best Western College Park Hotel, exactly seven minutes before the scheduled arrival time despite forty-five minutes worth of rest area and traffic delays.

"Impressive," Julian thought. "And I know just who she's trying to impress."

"We need to go use the little girls room, Julian," Lois said as she nodded to her new cohort in the driver's seat. You get a headcount and start collecting the kids' IDs for check in, we'll just be a minute.

"You're leaving me alone with all of them?"

"No worries Mr. D, I've got your backside. Tee hee," piped in perky Donna. "I'll help you."

"Great. Thanks, kid. Let's go, Tirana," Lois said.

The easy part was accounting for every last child. There hadn't been time for anyone to scatter. Figuring out whose bag was whose was quite a bit tougher. Donna's leopard print clamshell was easy enough to pick out, but that left almost two dozen mostly brown or blue duffles with no distinguishing features.

Donna had no problem offering and executing a solution that involved a considerable and very public invasion of privacy. It got the job done and Danny LaRue would hopefully achieve manhood having outlived the newly coined moniker "Spiderman Underpants."

Lois and Tirana took their sweet time, and when they finally rolled up, all the hard work had been done. Lois would have gone off with her new squeeze to service the bus if Julian hadn't finally put his foot down.

"Oh, no you don't, Lois. You're not leaving me alone again with all this going on."

"No worries, Mr. D, I'm here for you," Donna piped in, not helpfully.

"Well, thank you, Donna. That's very thoughtful," Lois offered as she turned to go.

Julian reached up to grab her shoulder and turn her back around.

"Not so fast."

Lois gave him a look, but she also turned to Tirana and shrugged.

"I'll see you in a minute, Tee. Mr. Dickerson here seems incapable of handling a couple of kids on his own."

"Whatever," Julian said.

More trouble lay ahead at the reservation desk. Apparently, the married teachers who were originally meant to be the chaperones had been assigned the Executive Suite. Therefore, the new chaperones remained assigned to that room. In truth, this wasn't a suite at all, but a single slightly larger room with a better view of the parking lot, a large desk wedged between the California King and the window and a complimentary bottle of spring water. Lois thought it made sense for Julian to take Tirana's room on the ground floor and, in turn, for Tirana to stay in the Suite with her. Julian thought not. What seemed reasonable to Julian was that Lois go and stay in Tirana's room if she wanted to be with Tirana so badly.

"But, Juli, that doesn't really make a lot of sense now. Think about it. We're two plus size gals with a wardrobe to match and all of the extra women's things like hair dryers and such that men just don't need."

"When's the last time you used a hairdryer, Lois? What would you even dry if you used a hairdryer? Your eyebrows? Because your eyebrows have more hair than your head."

"I'm sure Tirana, who as you rightly insinuate is more Fem has plenty of women's things, Julian, and besides, you're so little that the janitor's closet would be like a master suite for you. My God, you're one of the only men on earth who flies First Class in coach. Plenty of legroom for you, am I right? Just so long as little Julian is comfortable, everybody else can just squeeze in as best they can in life."

Arguing parties always gave Donna C. a sense of superiority and purpose; especially arguing adults and most especially if those adults happened to be two of her teachers. She prided herself on being an intuitive and highly effective referee. If you came from the family she came from, you'd be great at it too, she surmised.

"Ok you two, time out," she said and clapped her hands and stamped her feet to get their attention. "Shhhttt," she warned as Lois prepared to protest.

"Not another word, please. This is embarrassing. You two are supposed to be the chaperones here and look what you're so not acting like. Is this what you want your students to see or how you wish your legacy to be remembered by them?"

Lois and Julian were startled into attention as much by Donna's assertiveness as by her brain's twisting turn of phrase.

"First of all, I am proposing to you that we find out if there is more than one Executive Suite to be had and, if so, if it may very well be available and be able to help us end this knocking of heads against each other."

She turned to the somewhat cowering person behind the front desk and waited for the answer to the question she thought had been sufficiently asked.

When 'My name is Chessie' simply offered a blank stare. Donna inquired impatiently, "Well, do you or do you not have another suite, and if you do, may I spell it out? We would like to know if we can be accommodated within it."

"There's only one suite, currently, Maam," 'My name is Chessie' reported dutifully. "See the whole fourth floor is under renovation and…" Donna raised her hand in front of 'My name is Chessie''s face.

"Fine, enough, renovations are not of importance if that doesn't mean you have suitable rooms for business professionals and respected teachers such as these who have practically rented almost a whole floor of your rooms in this hotel."

Julian, Lois and 'My name is Chessie' averted their eyes as Donna paced a few steps forward and a few steps back, clearly conjuring her plan B.

Julian successfully called heads. Lois insisted on a do over and prevailed. Round three put Julian back up, but round four was again tails.

Just as 'My name is Chessie' was suggesting Rock, Paper, Scissors, Tirana returned to report that she had gathered the students from their respective quarters and had them waiting out front to board the bus and head for lunch at Olive Garden and then hit the Washington Monument and various war memorials.

"Just go ahead and put your stuff in the room and we'll figure all this out later."

She said after Donna apprised her, "C'mon, you're holding everybody up. It's just a room, we'll figure it out."

Julian stared out the window at the slightly suburban streets. It had started to rain and scattered pedestrians under cover of umbrellas, plastic bags, briefcases and ponchos swarmed under the protective wings of the bus shelters that punctuated the sidewalks. He identified with them even as he observed through the protective barrier of the thick glass. Most were solitary, but for an occasional mother with a small child. He remembered being a small child and a time when being small was a good thing.

Lois, who must have noticed his melancholy, offered him a handful of Good N Plenty. The pink and white capsules always struck him as slightly Valley of the Dolls and he considered accepting them even though he didn't like licorice.

"C'mon, Buddy. Why so glum? We're in Washington D.C.. It's gonna be nice. Our nation's capital. Give it a chance."

Julian shook his head and would have shuffled his feet, but they didn't quite reach the floor.

"Jules, Jules, Jules, what I said before that was just in the heat of the moment. You know how long it's been since I met anybody? I know it's a little sudden, but I've been sitting around waiting for this for seven, maybe eight, nine years. That's a hell of a long time, my friend, you have to admit, it's a long time to wait."

Julian shrugged and half nodded.

Lois took his face between her two big, soft as biscuit dough hands and turned his head toward her.

"Like I've said about a gazillion times, you're a good guy, Jules. You're my best pal, and believe me, there's no one, except maybe a pretty bus driver who might just be a momentary distraction anyways, that I would rather hang out with. I'm sorry if I hurt your feelings little buddy and for God sake don't take everything to heart like you do. I know you can be tough, Jules. Just look at how you're standing up to that bitch of a soon to be ex-wife. You're the man, Jules, a short man, yeah, but who cares? I'm here for you. I got your back."

"Sometimes, I just wish I had never been born, Lois. Or if I had to be born, Japan would have been best. In Japan, I'd be just another average guy in a drawer in the wall of a business hotel. I think that would feel great. I've always thought that would feel great."

"Hey, I'm sorry. You're a lot more of a man than you give yourself credit for. Now let's go and have a good lunch and lots of it."

Tirana eased the big bus into a space provided for such in the Olive Garden parking lot. The pneumonic braking system exhaled a satisfying hiss. Lois stood up and with her trusty field hockey megaphone pressed to her lips, announced the rules of engagement to a throng of previously distracted teens brought to attention by her booming voice. Julian and Tirana couldn't help but be impressed. She sure knew how to take command. "Masterful," they thought.

Julian really wanted the soup, salad and breadstick combo, but found himself ordering the more pricey Chicken Parm so as not to compromise the rare opportunity of not having to pay for his own lunch.

Donna, who sat with them, got what Julian had wanted and being the slightly presumptuous, but nonetheless thoughtful kid she was, snuck the trio of adults free side salads. Lois and Tirana might just as well have been dining al fresco on a private gondola in Venice because they were so enthralled by one another's company. Julian managed to satisfy himself with a surprisingly delicious meal and the nonstop chatter of his most devoted student.

"If you were to put Doris the Child wife in today's written literature, you might not have as good of an amount of receptiveness. Now there's all this Feminism, which I don't think of myself as, but a lot of people and especially women people do. What do you think, Mr. D, do I have a point here or am I just whistling at windmills as they say?"

"You have a point, Donna. Doesn't she have a point, ladies? Ladies?"

"Don't even bother trying at all, Mr. D, they are so not in a mood for a literary discussion such as us. They probably don't necessarily care even who Charles Dickens is much, less who his characters are. 'Been there, done that,' they could be saying right now."

"I think you may be right about that, Donna."

"Well thank you, thank you so very much for the things. It was so nice of you to say so. I don't have to always think it's just me having these ideas. More salad? Some breadsticks?"

The Cannoli Trio, Sicilian Cheesecake, Zeppoles and Tiramisu did not disappoint. Julian was even able to make light of the dollop of chocolate fudge he managed to drip on the front of his white shirt. He did have to draw the line at Donna cleaning it up for him.

It was with a huge sense of self importance that he scrutinized the check that was presented to him. Never before had he paid such an impressive restaurant bill. That said, it wasn't an unreasonable amount considering the size of the group. Meticulously calculating a fifteen percent gratuity to the penny, adding it to the total and signing with a flourish made him swell with pride. He threw down his credit card with feigned nonchalance knowing that Fitz would be reimbursing him, but that his lunch mates weren't necessarily aware of the fact.

As they gathered their doggy bags and coats, Julian felt light-headed and newly significant. For the first time that day, his sense of well being was restored. A few of the more well-mannered students came up to thank him personally. His response varied from "My pleasure" to "It was nothing."

Driver, chaperones and teenagers filled the bus that pulled out of the parking lot with a sugar high so palpable that the idea of visiting war memorials seemed gleefully uplifting. Then, it would come the crash.

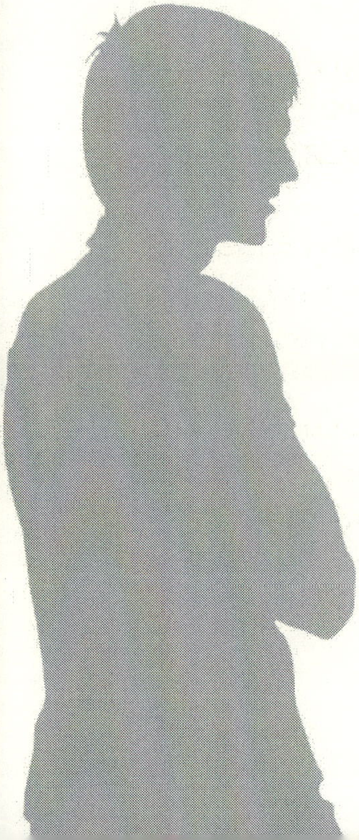

CHAPTER
Four

And it wasn't just a sugar crash.

The bus was moving along at a good clip though Tirana was exercising greater caution on the newly slick roads. Her heightened need to concentrate left Lois feeling a little neglected.

"There I go again with the instant codependence," Lois thought. "What the hell is my problem, anyways? I think I'm so tough and look at me, look at what happens to me when I meet a pretty girl."

Julian, sitting beside her, was soon lost in his own bout of self castigation. He scrolled through his phone, avoiding Social Media as he'd done since the boom dropped with Amanda. He had no appetite for her ubiquitous selfies and the egotistical captions that accompanied them. Who hearts their own picture, anyways?

There was an email from Dale Erlich, the attorney that Lois had insisted he hire to represent him in the divorce. Julian opened it reluctantly and quickly wished he hadn't.

Dear Mr. Dickerson,

I'm writing to inform you that your wife has brought emotional abuse charges against you and has asked local law enforcement to issue her a restraining order in an effort to legally evict you from the marital domicile. Not to worry. We'll fight these baseless accusations together. I'll need to see you at your earliest convenience and wish you a successful trip to Washington D.C. this weekend.

Yours truly,
Dale Erlich, Esquire

Julian's face flushed red from the neck up. Noticing this and thinking she might even detect steam coming from out of his ears, Lois took his shoulders in her hands and gave him a shake. Julian's gaze landed on her face and it was not a happy gaze.

"What the hell, Little Buddy, what is wrong with you? You still thinking about the Suite; you can have the Suite if it's that important to you. What do I care, keep the damn Suite, Juli."

Without a word, Julian passed his phone to Lois. She scanned the lawyer's letter and cursed sotto voce so as not to be overheard by the screaming students behind them, who wouldn't have heard a foghorn if it blew next to their earlobes, but Lois thought the occasion called for extra caution. She let out one of her long whistles and shook her head.

"That bitch!" she whispered. "Emotional abuse, is it? She's accusing YOU of emotional abuse? It doesn't get more ironical than that, my friend. Holy Mother of God, has the woman no shame? But Julie, Julie, Julie, lemme tell you, this is just another one of her dirty tactics to get the better of you and like Erlich says, we ain't gonna let her get away with it. She wants a fight, we'll give her....."

Suddenly the big bus swerved violently to the left. There was a faint thud and then it lurched sharply to the right, brakes screeching, glass shattering, tires skidding and kaboom, a kind of mind numbing, bottom falling out from beneath you thud accompanied by a brief sharp scream. The bus halted. In the ensuing surreal seconds of total silence, Julian realized he was on the floor. There was something big and heavy on top of him and he couldn't move. Once they began, the screams and shouts seemed as distant as the whining sirens and then louder and louder. His head was pounding and he couldn't see anything. He felt the weight on top of him shift and then lift off of him. The thing turned around and he could see that the bulk was his pal Lois. She reached for him, cradling his head in her big hands.

"Jule, Jule, you okay? Talk to me, Little Buddy, tell me you're okay, god dammit." Julian managed a thumbs up, the delivery of which caused significant pain. At this, Lois summarily let go of his head and disappeared.

Whatever else was going on around him, and Julian perceived it was something significant, he felt as if he was in his own little bubble. He couldn't feel much, but knew that if he tried to move at all, 'not much' quickly became 'too much.'

He registered the muscular arms of the handsome young EMT who was deftly shifting him onto a sheet of some kind.

"Don't worry, kid. We're going to make sure that you and your classmates are taken care of here. Try to stay calm. I'm going to try to move you and it may be a bit painful, but we'll get that sorted out in no time. Ya ready?"

Julian wanted so badly to tell this young whipper snapper that he was a grown adult, God dammit, not some teenage kid, but the words wouldn't come out. All he could do was blink enigmatically and brace for the predicted physical discomfort. As he was being manhandled out of his nest on the bus floor, the four letter words rushing to Julian's lips translated in the open air to mere grunts and groans. He felt his body being lifted up and set down on a hard, narrow bed. The sky, now divested of clouds, was just plain beautiful blue and the last thing Julian set eyes on until much had gone on without his awareness and the blue sky was replaced with a beige popcorn ceiling that loomed very much closer to his face than had that sky. He briefly panicked thinking maybe heaven was more institutional than he would have wished. With great trepidation, he directed his fuzzy gaze around the room. There were tubes and white sheets and linoleum tile and he could see that his knees were bent upwards and could not be moved. An intravenous bag hung beside him and he noted that he was attached to it by a narrow tube that disappeared under a bandage on his left arm. A little cuff on the index finger of his right hand was tethered to a machine of some kind with those scary doctor show scrolling digital graphs spiking ominously now and again. Amid the inscrutable beeps and whooshes, he detected the intermittent human words booming from a PA system. He located a beige plastic console on top of the thin blanket that covered him and pressed randomly at the buttons sending himself up and down, up and down at a terrifying velocity.

"Help!" he heard his own voice cry out. "Somebody help me!"

"Shut the hell up." The curtain surrounding the bed next to Julian's flew open.

He found himself staring at none other than Spiderman Underwear, who's left arm was encased in a large white cast.

"Mr. Dickerson. Sorry, ahhh, I had no idea... I thought it was just another kid."

A male nurse entered the room carrying a tray with little Styrofoam cups of individual serve waters with peel back aluminum tops.

"What's all the commotion, fellas?"

"Where am I, what happened, what the hell is going on around here?"

"Now, now, young man. It's okay, you were in an accident; you're going to be fine."

"But where am I?" Julian repeated.

"You're in the Pediatric wing of Medstar Hospital in Georgetown."

"Georgetown?"

"Yes, that's right, Washington D.C."

"The pediatric wing?"

"Well, yeah," Nurse Ronnie replied with a touch of attitude.

"Get me the hell out of here. I'm a full grown, adult, thirty one year old man, God dammit!"

"Oh dear," Ronnie intoned as he leaned into his walkie talkie to say "We have a live one in Room 202. Send back up please, requesting back up."

Nurse Ronnie's colleague arrived with a large syringe and held Julian's arm in place while he sunk a long needle into it and delivered whatever substance was inside.

Some hours later, Julian opened his eyes and immediately set upon the twin peaks of his knees. He instinctively tried to move them and found they would not cooperate. He turned his head and blinked at the reflection of himself and the gizmos to which he was attached. Through the big glass window, he peered into the cool, glossy, black night. He winced as a sharp spasm clenched his right calf and was just able to reach it to massage the pain away.

"I'm in a hospital in our nation's capital" registered in his brain.

"They have me in the children's ward" followed.

"Has Amanda been notified? Amanda, what a nice girl she seemed, in the beginning, before I had to go ahead and get married to her. What about Barcus? I hope my boy is okay. I hope he's with Mitch and not with the bitch." Julian smiled in appreciation of his unintended rhyme.

Somehow he intuited that if he squeezed the little thingamagig on his forefinger he would find relief and so he squeezed and slipped back into blissful thoughtlessness and sleep.

In the morning, he had the displeasure of pooping into a cold steel pan under the watchful gaze of Nurse Sandy McGuire. Clearly, she had done this sort of thing enough times to not appear in the least impressed with Julian's modesty, protestations or, finally, his bodily output. She deftly removed it and gave his bottom a wipe. Julian couldn't help but warm to her. She was so efficient and caring in her matter of fact sort of way. Julian felt he had possibly found himself an ally. "Nurse McGuire, I need your help."

"That's what they all say," McGuire responded with an assertive wink.

"No, really, there seems to have been a terrible mistake. You see, well it's probably quite obvious to you, I'm no child."

McGuire took a step backwards in a clear gesture of self defense.

"Hey, child or no child, kid, I'm not that kind of girl."

"No, no, no, no, that's not what I meant. What I meant is, they put me in the children's wing. This is the children's wing, yes? And, see, I'm a grown man. The boy in the next bed, that boy is my student. I teach tenth year English Lit. I can prove this. I just need my things, my wallet, my I.D."

McGuire peered at him with begrudging curiosity and picked up his chart. It says here you came in with the other juvenile victims of a tour bus accident; no identification."

"Oh God, please Nurse McGuire, you've got to help me here."

"You can call me Sandy."

"Well thank you, Sandy. My name is Julian, Julian Dickerson and I haven't been a juvenile for nearly two decades. I'm thirty-one and my name is Julian Dickerson and you've got to get me out of here."

"Ok, calm down, Julian, may I call you Julian?"

"Well, sure, of course you can."

"Listen, I'm inclined to believe you, although, I have to say, I can see how someone could have made an honest mistake."

"Yeah, I know, it's not the first time."

"Well, yeah, gee, I guess I believe you. But I'm just a lowly nurse around here, let me see if I can grab your doctor or I could go to the Dept. head, but she and I are not exactly on speaking terms at the moment. So that's not going to work, but the doctor is scheduled to come see you at 10 a.m. Until, then, do me a favor and sit tight."

As Julian watched Nurse McGuire, 'Sandy,' leave the room, he tried to calculate whether she was a tallish woman or a shortish woman. Tallish was the disappointing conclusion. He peeled back the foil tab on his little carton of juice and sipped from the tiny straw. He wasn't particularly hungry under the current circumstances, but he did manage one of the two institutional L'Eggos stacked on his plate and wished there was more maple syrup substitute.

The doctor didn't show up until after noon. Luckily Spiderman Underwear, aka Carmicheal, had finally awoken from his extenuated teenage slumber and was able to verify "Mr. Deckerly's" identity.

Julian expected that this would result in his immediate relocation to the appropriate adult facility, but there were yet some hurdles to jump. Julian, for obvious reasons, was not a fan of hurdles.

Hurdle Number One: The doctor thought it premature to move the patient in his present condition and would prefer that he stay put for at least a few more days.

Hurdle Number Two: There were no other beds available in the hospital, other than in Pediatric as it happened, at that particular moment.

Hurdle Number Three: Julian's unusual case would need to be taken up with the Head of the Department and McGuire having recused herself, it was on Dr. Pope; but Pope's schedule was such that he doubted he'd be able to execute the outreach until sometime the following morning.

Before sinking completely back into self-pity, self-loathing and despair, Julian knew enough to squeeze the morphine drip that promised a sweet reprieve. "So I have a broken knee and a fractured spine and I'm in the Pediatric Ward because I'm so God damm short, but hey, could be worse. Feeling pretty good, matter of fact, matter o'facto, matfacto, mattafatta, muddafucka, yahahahahah..." whereupon he fell into a deep slumber.

All Julian could remember about the nightmare was that Amanda was in it and Barcus, and Barcus was under Amanda's spell somehow and it was terrifying. He screamed and flailed and pulled out his intravenous and tried to stand up out of the bed so he could run for his life.

"Help, get me out of here, get me out of here!" he screamed.

Nurse Ronnie ran into the room, put his giant hands around Julian's shoulders and assertively lowered him back down onto his pillows. His orderly sidekick, Robin to his Batman, fussed with the intravenous. Ronnie held Julian down and told him to breathe.

"I know, I know, we had a bad dream, did we? Alright Mr. Dickerson, alright. I know, now. Just try to breathe, calm down, you're alright. Everything's going to be alright."

"You, you didn't even believe me when I told you I wasn't a child," Julian managed between air hungry gasps.

"No, I did not, I did not believe you and for that I am very, very sorry. I'm sorry, Mr. Dickerson. You believe me, don't you? I'm sincerely sorry... Friends?"

Julian's response was a diffident shrug.

"Andrew, wasn't I just telling you about Mr. Dickerson here and how badly I felt about not taking him seriously last night?

Andrew can tell you. We were just discussing it, weren't we, Andrew?"

"That's right, Boss."

Ronnie turned to Julian, like a prosecutor who had just deposed his star witness. "See that? Now do you forgive me?"

Julian figured he wasn't in much condition to continue the struggle so he gave Ronnie a tepid thumb up accompanied by a surreptitious eye roll in Andrew's direction intended to enlist the sidekick's confidence and future support if needed.

"Well good, good then. I'm only here to help you. Now tell me, when is the last time you evacuated your bowels?"

Julian was awakened the next morning by the tight assed, buttoned up, Head of the Department. He had hoped the person entering his rather public accommodations was Sandy, but the Department Head was no Sandy. She wasn't Sandy-like in the least little way.

The Department Head was accompanied by Dr. Pope and an impossibly tall and skinny gentleman who was introduced as the lead legal counsel for the Hospital. Both men kept as much distance from the Department Head as the tight quarters would allow. Julian could easily imagine why.

"Mr. Dickerson," she began with a smile that revealed her dazzling white, slightly oversized set of precision teeth.

Julian surmised that the teeth were no more real than the smile.

"I'm sure I speak for all of us here at Medstar when I extend the sincerest of apologies for this regrettable mistake. Had you arrived with any sort of identification, I assure you, things would have gone quite differently. That said, however, I must stand by the excellent and perhaps life-saving care that was administered to your benefit by physicians and staff alike.

We understand that you're upset, but ask that you join us in directing your attention to the bigger picture."

She paused and waited for what she expected to be Julian's gracious response, when none came she turned to her attorney.

"Please explain to Mr. Dickerson here that the hospital performed emergency services in good faith and that we have no exposure here for making an honest mistake."

"She speaks the truth, Mr. Dickerson. Though this little problem—teehee—that's funny, I said, 'little problem', get it? Little?"

Pope jabbed the poor fellow as both the Department Head and Julian, in a momentary show of like-minds, glared at the guy.

"Uhh, sorry, just trying to make a little, ah, a silly joke. Lawyers should never try to make jokes. At least not this lawyer. Ha."

"Suffice it to say, the hospital, as my colleague rightly pointed out, acted in good faith, Mr. Dickerson. And while an apology is in order, we accept no formal liability for any of the actions taken on your behalf. Any questions?"

"When are you planning on getting me the hell out of here?"

Taking her cue to try some levity, the Department Head said, "The only current availability is in the maternity ward, Mr. Dickerson. Now we don't think you'll be much happier in the maternity ward. Haha!"

Her laugh was shrill and abrupt like that of a proper doyenne being goosed at a cocktail party.

Even if what she said had been the least bit funny, and Julian thought it was not, it would have been instantly disqualified by that laugh.

"No, really, I jest. We are working on it, Mr. Dickerson. Honestly, all resources have been deployed and we are doing our level best. In the meantime, Dr. Pope here has advised that it really is best that you not be moved prematurely so it's kind of a win-win."

Julian clearly didn't share her concept of what a win-win was and expressed as much by the terrible sneer he mustered for her benefit.

"Well, I think we're done here. We'll be in touch about your new accommodations, Mr. Dickerson, and don't you be afraid to contact us if there's anything at all we can do to make your stay more tolerable."

The Department Head backed away from Julian's bed as she spoke. Her high heel snagged an electrical cord on the ground and she tripped and fell backwards into the arms of the skinny lawyer who was able to catch her, but not able to prevent himself from falling backwards and crashing through the swinging door into the hallway. Julian laughed out loud while poor Dr. Pope tried to hold it in until, by the sounds of it, the two had picked themselves back up and stumbled down the hallway.

Nurse Sandy McGuire was a breath of fresh air, but not a bearer of good tidings. She reported that getting Julian moved was priority number one, but still nothing suitable had opened up. Upon hearing this, Julian expressed to her how humiliating this and many other experiences in his life had been and how very much he wished, not to be tall even, but just to be normal height. Taking his cue, Sandy also got a bit more personal in her conversation with her patient and told him all about her fiancé, a firefighter, and by the looks of it, a tall, strapping, good looking guy who had once weighed over three hundred pounds.

"So, you see, change is possible."

"I appreciate your encouraging words, but I'm afraid there is no Jenny Craig for shortness."

With this, Julian's heart descended a floor or two. Sandy, who really was ideally wrought for her care-giving profession, couldn't help but see his point and regretted that her attempt at lifting his spirits had failed so miserably.

"So you're a little on the short side," she said. "But I know guys who would kill for that head of hair. Height is one thing, but look at how handsome you are, look at those green eyes. I know a lot of women who would fall for those green eyes alone. Look, Julian, God works in really weird ways, ya know? Maybe you wound up here in order to learn some kind of lesson, like it's better to be short and ambulatory than tall and confined to a wheelchair. And, hey, if they hadn't put you in the wrong wing, you and I would never have met. And I am the nicest nurse in the whole place. I can guarantee you."

Julian found this reassurance so sweet and yet so depressing at the same time.

"What a woman," he thought. "The one that got away."

Nurse Ronnie reaffirmed Nurse Sandy's complimentary impression by obviously flirting with Julian later that evening.

"Here we go again with the gay guys," Julian thought, but he had to admit it was flattering.

The next morning, a flurry of aids and techs arrived to move Julian to the adult Orthopedic wing of the hospital. He would have said goodbye to Spiderman Underpants, but the kid was sleeping in as usual.

As he was being wheeled down the corridor, Julian spotted Nurse McGuire. She turned from her conversation with the Department Head and gave him a wink. Julian considered that his stay in the children's wing hadn't been all bad after all. It was no surprise to him that Lois was his first visitor.

"What took you so long?" Julian asked.

"Well, Mr. Big Stuff, if you hadn't left your damn wallet at Olive Garden maybe we all wouldn't have thought you just disappeared into thin air. Did you ever think about that?"

"There was a lot going on, Lois. And I was not aware that I was about to be thrown on the floor of a bus and crushed by a giant P.E. teacher. Maybe then I would have made sure to remember my wallet."

"Hey, I didn't crush you. Me falling off my seat on account of a bus crash is what crushed you, Julie. So technically, it wasn't my fault."

"How's everyone else? I know that Carmicheal has a busted arm, but otherwise, he seems good."

"Carmicheal?"

"Spiderman Underwear."

"Oh, him."

"Well, most of the kids are fine. Donna is fine. Tirana, thank God, is okay. She's got whiplash, but other than that… And little Sonia, the trouble maker, looks like she's gonna make it. It was touch and go there for a while, but she's a real fighter, that one."

"Sonia?"

"Well, that's what I've decided to call her."

"Wait, what? Who's Sonia?"

"Oh right, I guess you hadn't heard. Sonia is the little rascal who caused the whole mess in the first place. The cat? The cat that ran in front of the bus and made Tirana swerve so as not to hit her? You with me?"

"All of this so as not to hit a cat? What the hell, Lois, a cat?"

"Hey, we all know you're a dog person, Julian, but cats can be amazing companions too. You have to have one and then you get to experience it. Don't put down cats until you've had one of your own, please. It's more one on one than dogs, but just as meaningful."

"I can't believe that I'm lying here in this hospital in our nation's capital, not even in the local hospital where we live, because of a damn cat. Jesus, Lois."

"You just don't get it, do you?"

"No, Lois, no I don't."

"How long you in for?"

"Apparently, my left knee is busted up pretty badly. They say the cast will be on at least through the summer and then we'll see. And then, there's the matter of the spine. I'm like the bionic man, Lois. I have enough titanium in me to set off an airport alarm at roadside check-in. I swear to God."

"I'm gonna have to break it to Shelley."

"Your daughter? Break what to her?"

"Yes, my daughter. Break it to her that her prom date is going to be a no show."

"I guess every cloud has a silver lining."

"Don't be a wise ass, please."

"Sorry."

"No tennis for a while then?"

"No tennis. How's Barcus?"

"Mitch tells me Barcus is doing just great. He even gives him credit for business picking up some. He says your dog has a way with people. He's a good distraction, so's the lowlifes don't have to just sit there and think about how miserable they have it."

"That's my boy."

"It was my distinct displeasure to notify your bitch for a soon to be ex-wife that there had been an accident and that you were missing."

"How did she react?"

"She said you probably ran from the scene like the chicken shit you are and if you should happen to turn up let her know so she could take the yellow ribbons off the trees in your neighborhood."

"What a bitch."

"What were you thinking, Jules?"

"She was nice for a minute. We had really, really, really good sex. She seemed to like me for who I was. I don't know, Lois, I guess I was thinking a lot of things."

"Or maybe you weren't thinking at all, my friend. That's my theory, you were letting your dick do the thinking."

"Hey, that is so crude even for you, Lois."

"Oh, gee whiz, sorry I triggered your delicate sensibilities, my friend. Sometimes, the truth is not pretty. So why try to sugarcoat it?"

Julian gave a little squeeze to his morphine dispenser.

"A friggin cat, really, Lois?"

"The cat has a name, Julie. Her name is Sonia and I can only wish it would have been your wife under the wheel of that bus. We all would have been better off."

"Amen to that."

Days later, when Julian finally met Lois's new pet Sonia, he'd recognize that she bore an undeniable almost exact resemblance to the kitten in the Hang in There poster, which was the first thing Julian saw when he awoke in the pediatric ward after his surgery. It had served as an early tip that his situation was off. That and the cartoon giraffe motif of his bed curtains.

"Jesus."

Julian spent the following days getting reacquainted with the likes of Ellen and Oprah. He normally would have opted for WWF, but found that, with the pain still throbbing in his hoisted leg, any violent physical reference was more than he could bear.

Nurse Sandy came to visit as often as possible and helped to occupy the empty space in Julian's lonely heart. His private room was relatively deluxe, way better than the Executive Suite at the Best Western that he would or would not have been accommodated in. All good, he supposed, though he found himself getting wistful even for the proximity of his mostly slumbering former roommate, Carmichael, aka Spiderman Underwear.

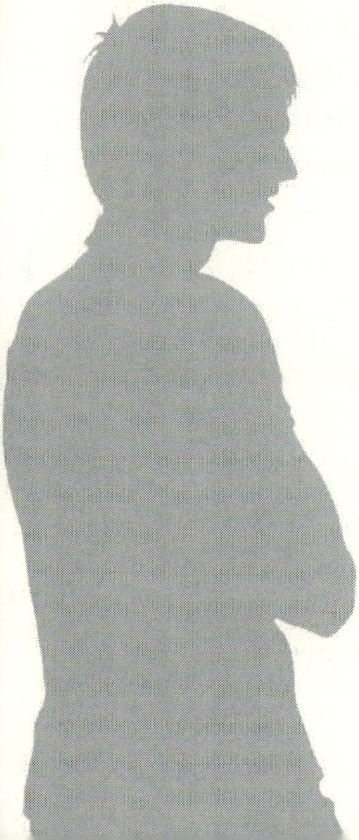

CHAPTER
Five

When the day finally arrived for his transfer to the hospital in Springfield, he felt somewhat like the little boy he was so often mistaken to be. Goodbye to Nurse Sandy was tough; she had been so kind to him. He would even miss Nurse Ronnie, who'd proven to be sweetly attentive if not overly so. (Nothing he could do about it, he was irresistible to a certain type of gay man and Ronnie was clearly that type.) Julian wished he could have played God just this once and swapped out Sandy's sisterly devotion for Ronnie's lustier version.

Though Julian swore he'd remain in touch with his newfound friends, he knew deep down that such vows were rarely kept. He would receive Sandy and her husbands' Christmas greetings far into the future and thereby be given an opportunity to observe their growing family enjoying seemingly idyllic lives filled with fun and adventure.

Julian's ambulance ride from D.C. back to Massachusetts was almost as speedy as the bus trip there with Tirana at the wheel, almost. The new home for him and his busted knee and back was not the warm patient friendly style of institution he'd grown accustomed to. The Weldon Rehabilitation Center of Mercy Hospital was a cold (literally freezing cold) facility where efficiency was the touchstone and the only mercy was expressed with terse politeness. At least, Julian could have visitors. Lois came just about every day, and even Mitch showed up once or twice. A process server made his way in as well and deposited a restraining order from his devoted wife.

"How the hell did she get a restraining order against a guy who is stuck in traction in a shithole hospital for weeks and weeks?" Lois wanted to know.

"That's Amanda for you. She probably cozied up to the head detective. That would be her M.O."

"Well, the good news is it doesn't look like you're getting out of here any time soon, Buddy."

"What's good about it? If I don't get out of here soon, I'm going to lose my mind, Lois. And when I do get out, then what?"

"Well, I'm afraid to tell you, my friend, we got bigger problems than your bitch ex-wife, almost ex. I'm afraid you and I are out of a job, at least that's how it's looking."

"What the hell, Lois. Exactly what are you saying to me?"

"I didn't want to bring it up any sooner than I had to, with you stuck here in this god awful place as is, but the whole bus crash thing, there's a lot of angry parents who are looking for someone to blame. And they're not just stopping at you and me, Pal. They're taking it all the way to the top. I don't think it's unrealistic to say that the future of Fitz Prep is in jeopardy and not looking so good."

"Oh, so we're the scapegoats, huh. Well, welcome to the club, Lo. Welcome to my world. Any other great news?"

"Just that Mitch's business has been improving steadily and he's thinking of renaming the place Barcus' Bar... with your permission, of course. Oh, and I'm working the kitchen pretty good, simple fare, but reliable, you know? Tirana is my secret weapon, since she does all of the actual cooking. I just make sure it gets heated up and served to the customers. And Sonia..."

"Sonia who?"

"The cat, Julian, Sonia the cat. She and your dog are getting along great. I think it might be a love connection."

"Oh, geez!"

Despite the always stimulating visits with Lois, Julian was exceedingly bored. When he found he was able to sign up to see a counselor once a week, he set aside his negative feelings about the efficacy, indeed the manliness of therapy and figured what the heck.

Mrs. Stuart was a tall, wispy lady who had retired from Social Service work and now offered solace and support on a volunteer basis to those long term patients in need. Her tenure at Mercy had been brief enough that Julian was actually her first ever client.

She was anxious to make a good showing and listened with visible intensity to every word that fell from Julian's lips. She kept a packet of tissues in her large purse for vulnerable moments and Julian was grateful for this on those occasions when his self-pity was simply more than he could bear. Stuart provided peppermints too, which reminded Julian of his Granddad, God rest his soul.

Mrs. Stuart exercised the greatest patience with her client and so met his resistance to opening up in any meaningful way. As such, it had taken weeks before those tissues were brought into service, but once they were, oh brother! As Julian warmed to the process of sharing his deepest, darkest secrets with this stranger and revealing his most profound disappointments and greatest dreams, he began to find a new flicker of hope. She cared, he could tell, she really did, and Julian could not repress a huge smile when Stuart suggested that they meet twice a week rather than just the one.

"I'm not all that busy yet," she confessed. "And I suspect you could use the extra time."

Further evidence that Julian was not so alone in the world, after all, arrived in the form of a letter that was delivered one morning in mid-July. The pink envelope had a powerful floral smell that equally infused the pages within. It was necessary for Julian to borrow a surgical mask from an orderly so his nose was blocked as he read Donna's strange, but considerate missive.

> Dear Mr. D,
>
> There is an old song, an Oldie, that my mother still loves to listen to on her Sirius XM radio in her car. Although, just between you and between me, I don't think it is safe for her to be driving. Anyways, the song is 'Mr. D, oh Mr. D,' and she loves it and can remember some of the words and the tune. But, of

course, me, I can't remember it because I'm too young, but it did give me the idea to turn my thought to my teacher of the same name and I'm sorry to understand that, as I write this to you, you are still in the hospital from what happened when we had the bus accident in Washington, D.C. Well, that was quite a class trip experience, wasn't it? And now, I too enjoy the song about Mr. D even though it is not exactly the latest hit.

I hope that you are feeling better and I do not really know what is going on with our school. I hear that some of the parents are red hot hopping mad because they think this should have never happened and could have been prevented by better planning and more supervision on the parts of the people in charge, which would have been you and Miss Lois, but they think there should have been at least two more adults, in addition to the two you already were.

My parents feel happy that I was not hurt and that my helping out so much at the scene and being a good explainer of all that happened to the authorities in charge made me more popularly regarded than anyone thought I was in the past. I will return to school, if school is there to return to, as someone more liked. I've been called a students' student by one of the local newspapers, which maybe you have seen if you read the papers in the hospital. Of course, you must read them because what else is there to do in a hospital? I don't want to tell you too much about my own summer vacation because what if you decide to have that as one of our first assignments?

And I'm not even joking, I really think it could happen and how many times do you want to read the same old story even though it's pretty interesting, if I can say so myself.

Hint: my mother ended up back in what my Dad calls the Laughing Factory and I had to take care of dinner and such things. So much for Women's Liberation, right? Well, without giving everything away to you, I'll just say we had a lot of Domino's pizza and everyone seemed to like it so maybe that's some Women's Liberation right there in the long run.

But, don't worry, there are many other things for my essay, which you might be assigning. But, no, I have not been able to decide what I want to be when I grow up. A teacher? Maybe, but you'd probably say not even to think *about it because look where it got you in the hospital for the entire summer.*

I don't know if you follow politics. I've decided not to because it will remind me of our nation's capital, Washington D.C., and as you know, that is where we had our bus crash.

Please write back to me if you are not too busy lying in bed all day and maybe reading a newspaper or two and perhaps some literature, which I know you love and watching any TV. Hey, even though that sounds like more than I thought, a letter to me would be great.

Sincerely yours,

Your best student Donna C.

Julian marveled, as usual, at Donna's unique turn of phrase and overall bastardization of the English language. He did not get around to writing her back. She'd guessed correctly that he did read the local papers and was familiar with her elevation to student hero status. Quotes such as, "I just did what any responsible teenage girl would do without ever having been in a bus accident, which just had to have been on a class trip with her school when it happened"

She was credited for saving the lives of many, though no one's injury had been anywhere close to fatal.

The papers loved a good hero story he supposed.

When young Sean Tibbets cub reporter for The Yankee Tattler and author of many a Donna C. hero profile, came to interview him for his Follow Up In the News column, Julian was grateful that he was unable to refute or verify the legend of "best student" and Fitz Preps newly minted Joan of Arc. He'd been unconscious from the moment of the crash. Tibbets was disappointed that his eye-witness was no witness at all while Julian was insulted to find that his own injuries and trauma were of little to no interest to the reporter.

Apparently, this was all about Donna and so Julian grudgingly responded to Tibbets wide ranging inquiries.

'Could Julian have predicted the heroism that was demonstrated by his young 'protégé?'

"Protégé?"

"Well, everyone I've talked with has described her as your favorite student. Is 'protégé' not an accurate descriptive?"

Though Julian considered setting the record straight, he succumbed to what he rightly perceived to be a popular fever for the beatification of Donna C., teen superhero and so he let it slide.

Tibbet's article ran on the front page a day later with the headline; "Donna C's Brave Response To Tragedy No Surprise to Injured Teacher"

"I thought you told me they were coming to write a piece about you. What happened here, Juli?" Lois asked as she skimmed Julian's copy of The Tattler. "What the hell?"

"The hell is, Lois, that all anybody is interested in is Donna. To tell you the truth, I don't even care."

"What happened to standing up for yourself, Jules?"

"Well, I guess since I can't even stand, Lois, that option is out the proverbial window."

"You know I hate it when you talk like that, Julian, thinking you can throw around your big words and get no argument out of me. Well, I happen to know what proverbial means, little man, and not being able to stand up physically is no excuse anyway."

"It's just a damn newspaper article, my large friend."

"What did you call me?"

"You called me little man."

"Okay, okay, truce, peace, enough with the name calling. I have some important business to discuss with you. Something that could set us both up for life, Jules. I'm not kidding, for life!"

Juli was cautious at first. Not only did he have a very unhappy history with all things involving lawyers, his sense of loyalty, of being a standup guy who could roll with the punches and still have your back, of being a bigger man, if you will, than he appeared was all being put to the test.

"Don't be such a whus, Jules. This is a chance of a lifetime. You think Sebastian Fitzgerald the Third or Fourth or whatever the hell number Sebastian Fitzgerald he is or his father or any of the other Sebastian Fitzgerald's of any number gives a shit about you or me? They just want to throw us under the bus. Get it, throw us under the bus? Tirana came up with that one. She's the total package, Jules. Smart, beautiful, nice and funny as hell, but don't get me started. Anyways, she's all for it. Go after them with everything you've got is her opinion."

Jules picked at the fraying edge at the top of his cast. Unraveling the threads had become a means of focusing and in a symbolic way, Julian thought, of bringing him one tiny bit closer to freedom.

"She might be all that, Lois, but does this mean she's some authority on going up against a family that owns half of the county and then some. She some kind of legal savant now?"

"I don't know if she's any savant, Julian, and I'll have you show a little more respect, if you don't mind. I'm here offering you a chance to have it all, to never have to answer to the witless son of the dumb luckiest man in town, whose own great grandfather just happened to see a future in bootleg liquor at the right moment in history. We can do this, Jules. We don't have to just roll over like good little puppies and spend the rest of our lives with somebody else' slippers in our mouths."

"I'm not convinced, Lo. This is a big decision. Trust me, I'd love to get out from under the Sebastian Fitzgerald's of the world, but this is not a thing to be taken lightly, my friend. Yes, we could maybe, by some David and Goliath miracle, come out on top, but if we lose? If we lose, we're screwed for life. We'll never get hired by any educational institution again. In fact, nobody in any field of commerce would touch us with a ten foot pole."

"Who the hell is David and Goliath?"

"They're from the Old Testament."

"My parents weren't religious."

"Were they atheists?"

"Good question."

"Are you an atheist?"

"I'm not sure what I am, Jules, now quit changing the subject for God's sake."

Julian had much to ponder hours later when he was finally able to wear Lois down and/or she needed to go eat. Their debate had taken innumerable twists and turns, but Lois' pole vaulting metaphor, repeated several times in the conversation, seemed to underpin her most compelling angle on the subject. Julian couldn't get it out of his mind. He could see himself, little Julian, soaring over the heads of a roaring crowd to land softly and triumphantly in the lap of luxury. Tempting, tempting indeed.

The room in which this pondering and fantasizing occurred, and in which Julian had found far too much time to harken back to a disappointing and immutable past, was prison-like. The cinderblock walls and the metal bed and adjoining tray gave off a chill that could not be fully absorbed, if absorbed at all, by the one soft thing, a vinyl upholstered armchair meant to make visitors welcome but not too welcome. The one window was too high to peer out of; at least it was too high for Julian to peer out of.

It occurred to Julian more than once that evening that the very bed he reclined in was purchased by the indulgence of one Sebastian Fitzgerald Sr. After all, it was the Sebastian Fitzgerald Wing. And so, it was only after verifying that the solicitous Mrs. Stuart was scheduled to arrive next morning for another therapy session that Julian allowed himself to sink into his accustomed fitful slumber."

"Let's go back to this pole vaulting, Julian. I think there's something there."

Julian noted how much he loved Mrs. Stuart's way of challenging him to remain focused on the important things.

"I wish they had offered it at my high school. I think for a short person it would have been very empowering and I feel I would have been really pretty good at it."

"Go on."

"I really don't have anything else. That's it. I just wish my high school had offered pole vaulting and that I would have taken it up and been really good at it or..."

"Or what?"

"Or that I had been a normal height kid."

Mrs. Stuart smiled benevolently and nodded her head up and down, "Yes, yes, yes."

"What? Why you nodding?"

"This is what we therapists call a breakthrough, Julian. You may not know it or feel it in this very moment, but I can't emphasize enough how very encouraged I am. I'll look forward to seeing you on Thursday, and Julian, I think you're more of a pole vaulter than you give yourself credit for. Hug?"

Hugging Mrs. Stuart was so unlike hugging Lois. Julian's arms actually overlapped in the back and he needed to be conscious of not squeezing so hard that the dear old girl would break. One Lois hug equaled about half a dozen Mrs. Stuart hugs and always made Jules fear asphyxiation. Nonetheless, a hug was a hug, he thought, and he wasn't one to be turning down any one of those.

"Human contact was spare in this particular institution," Jules thought longingly of Nurse Sandy whose smile was better than any embrace.

The new addition to Julian's support team was Manny Menuda. Manny's well weathered skin was wrapped so tightly around his spry, muscular frame that, from the neck down and a five foot remove, he could easily have been mistaken for a twenty year old. Manny's appearance startled, puzzled and confused Julian, but once he got to know the pathology of this lifelong fitness fanatic, it all fell into place. Manny was petite, like him, but his presence was so non-stop Energizer Bunny that he filled any given space about as comprehensively as the air itself.

Julian liked Manny and admired his tenacity, but also feared the pace this little firecracker would inevitably dictate notwithstanding for one little minute the agonizing pain he put his client through. If there was anything, anything at all, Julian could do to avoid his so-called therapeutic sessions with Manny, Julian seized it. But there wasn't much. Manny was not one to abide excuses. He was a taskmaster who truly believed in the necessity of pain to achieve gain. The hospital Physical Therapy facility was a veritable torture chamber under his supervision. His words of encouragement were no less imposing.

"What, you gonna be a little pussy. You gonna cry, now like a leetle baby boy? Oh whah, whah, whah. You wanna get better or you wanna stay in bed for the rest of your life like a big baby? Huh, huh, I can't hear you, Julie. Is that what I'm gonna have to call you now? Julie, like a leetle girl? Does the leetle girl Julie have to take a leetle break? We gonna have a tea party, a princess party for leetle girl Julie? You want a leetle pink ribbon to put in your pretty leetle curls? Is that what you want?"

It kind of worked. Julian would become so enraged by Manny's non-stop insults that it gave him superhuman strength. On the occasion of a Lois hug, she noticed how Manny's unpleasant mode of training was actually producing results.

"What the hell? Is that a bicep I feel? Roll up your sleeve lemme see, lemme look at you, Jules. You getting muscles?"

Julian did his best to appear modest, but he couldn't help seeing himself just for a moment, attacking the track, planting his pole and launching himself over the heads of the adoring crowd.

"Uh, yeah, a little bit, I guess. You know I've been working out with Manny."

"I gotta meet this Manny guy, Julian. Seeing as we're in a similar line of work. I'd love to pick his brains if you know what I mean. You set it up?"

"Sure, sure, Lois. I'll see what I can do."

"Meanwhile, Mr. Six Pack, back at the ranch house, Snodgrass, tells us he has not had the pleasure of you responding to any of his calls or making an appointment to see him."

"Snodgrass?"

"The lawyer, Julian. Snodgrass the lawyer. The guy who is going to make you, well, let's see, a little bit rich? No. Super rich, Julian. Snodgrass who's going to make you and me and Tirana and not your ex-wife Amanda stupid money rich, like never have to work another day in your life rich, my friend."

"Oh, that guy."

"Yes, that guy, Jules. When you gonna meet with him or do I need to strap you to this hospital bed and drag him in here?"

"I'll meet with him, alright? I'll meet with him. This is a big decision, Lois. Like I said, it's one big roll of the dice and if I'm a little worried about it, shoot me. Like I told you before, we've got to go into this eyes wide open. We could lose everything, Lois, I mean everything!"

"Well, listen to Mr. Doom and Gloom who hasn't even spoken with our legal counsel as of yet and already knows all there is to know about it, you plan on living the rest of your life hiding behind your mama's apron strings, Julian?"

"You're kidding, right, my mama's apron strings? What the hell, Lois. I can assure you my mother never wore an apron in her life and you're starting to sound like Manny."

"Good, that's good if I sound like Manny. You need some Manny sounding people in your corner. With people like me and Manny, Julian you can be a winner for a change. Wouldn't that be just the best, Julie? You winning for a change? Why shouldn't you ever be a winner? Are the Amanda's and the Fitzgerald's of the world the only ones supposed to ever win anything? This is our chance, Julie. This is the opportunity of a lifetime. Your lifetime, my lifetime, Tirana's lifetime, all of those lifetimes. Just think about it, my friend."

Julian agreed to meet with Snodgrass. He really didn't feel he had a choice. Their appointment happened to fall on the same day that he received a call from his divorce attorney informing him that Amanda had sold the house to her mother for ten dollars and had expressed a willingness to split the proceeds with Julian despite the fact that she was under no legal obligation to do so.

"No, you're not on the deed and I believe it may be difficult for you to prove that you contributed anything at all to the mortgage, which was also in Amanda's name. At this point, and I hate to say this, Julian, I suggest you sign those papers and cut bait. There's really nothing left to fight for."

Initially, upon hearing this news, Julian was crest fallen, but his mind quickly drifted to a much more satisfying place. He considered how thoroughly pissed off Amanda would be if he won a huge settlement in a lawsuit with the Fitzgerald's and she stood to get none of it.

Snodgrass arrived to find a future client in a vengeful frame of mind and easily dismissed Lois's warnings that he would have to do a big sell job.

Julian was pretty much in the 'where do I sign?' mode. It mattered not at all that he found Snodgrass snarky and condescending. Rather have this guy on our side while Snodgrass laid out an aggressive strategy to fleece the venerable institution in who's employ Julian had spent the last four years of his life.

"Who knew this would be your year of the legal?" Lois wanted to know.

She asked this as she looked up from a document serving Julian for dereliction of duties as chaperone of the Fitz Prep Class trip to Washington D.C. The plaintiff was none other than Fitz Prep itself. Clearly, this was their strategy to deflect guilt for their own negligence.

"You get one of these?"

"Nope. I guess they're going after the big fish."

"The big fish?"

"Well, you were the senior staff, Julian, I'm just the lowly PE teacher. You were the one calling the shots. And according to eyewitnesses, you abandoned the scene."

"Abandoned the scene? Abandoned the scene?"

"Well, cool down now, Jules. I know you were out cold and being carted off and that if anyone has an ax to grind here it's you being holed up in this institution like you've been all summer long and losing your home, not to mention your job, and very possibly the full use of your left leg. But, however, even though all of this should be able to be proved, the fact still remains you, not me, were supposed to be in charge."

"No, Lois. No,no,no. We were in charge, Lois, you and me. One male chaperone and one female chaperone. We were in charge equally, and besides, we did nothing wrong. It says there that we neglected our duties. Neglected our duties? I for one was so hyper focused on looking out for those kids that I went and left my damn wallet at Olive Garden. Did you leave your wallet at Olive Garden, Lois?"

"Hey, Cowboy, save that fire for the judge. So, you left your wallet. Did I leave my wallet, no. Why? Because it's the person in charge who pays the bills, isn't it? Isn't, it, Jules?"

"First of all, Lois, I hate it when you call me cowboy."

"Oh, would you prefer Cowman, Jules? Is that better? Can I call you Cowman?"

"I'm not talking about the boy part, Lois, geez. Just don't call me cow anything, okay? It makes no sense, no sense at all. So, please just don't."

"Okay, okay, Jules, no harm intended, I swear to God. I think this whole sitting around here twiddling your thumbs is getting under your skin."

"Yes, Lois, I think so too. That and losing my home and my job and getting sued for something I had absolutely no control over. God, I can't wait to get the hell out of here."

"That'll be soon enough, my friend. What they say, another week or two?"

"That's what they say, but they said that three weeks ago."

"Yeah, but, I got a good feeling about it this time, Jules. Manny is doing wonders with your physical conditioning. Your shrink, Stuart? I think Stuart has a ways to go. Now, deal those cards. I'm feeling lucky today."

Julian shuffled, dealt and turned his attention to his hand to consider his strategy for beating Lois yet again.

By the time the aforementioned Mrs. Stuart arrived for their regularly scheduled appointment, Lois had accused him of cheating at least half a dozen times and claimed this is why he had won seventeen out of twenty three games.

"Mrs. Stuart! Not a minute too soon," Lois said as she threw down her pair of twos and got up to go.

"Royal flush," Julian announced as he laid his hand, card by card down, on the side of his bed.

"Well, good for you, Mr. Bigstuff. I'm out of here. Are you comin? Oh, that's right. You aren't going anywhere just yet, are you?"

"Don't be a sore loser, Lois."

"Whatever."

Julian was just as happy to focus his ensuing therapy session on the subject of his friendship with Lois whom Mrs. Stuart found "a little rough around the edges."

"Her heart is bigger than her mouth," Julian concluded and "I like it that she keeps me on my toes."

"You're both very special, Dear, each in your own way. I suspect that this is what drew you to one another."

"Makes sense to me."

That roughness around Lois's edges was on full display the following day when she barged into Julian's room waving her own notice of service.

"You were right. Now they're coming after both of us. What the hell, Jules? We were just trying to do the best job possible under the difficult circumstances that were no fault of our own. Doesn't that count for anything? What the hell is this world coming to?"

"The world isn't coming to anything, Lois. The world is the world, same as yesterday and pretty certainly same as tomorrow. But, cheer up, old pal, at least we have each other. We're gonna fight this together. And, besides, I got Snodgrass on the phone and he practically laughed the whole thing off. We've got nothing to worry about."

"Snodgrass said that?"

"Yes, that is exactly what Snodgrass said."

"You call me, Old Pal?"

"Yes, yes I guess I did."

"Huh."

"We good?"

"I think we're good."

Never one to ignore a solid lead, Sean Tibbets, cub reporter, made a subsequent visit to Julian's hospital retreat to get the scoop on the latest legal entanglements in the endlessly titillating case of the Fitz Prep class trip bus accident. His recent faithful recording of Headmaster Fitzgerald's view of the facts of the case, and the degree to which that good man's statements had slanderized Julian and Lois, had been the talk of the town. The fact that the Yankee Tattler had added several new subscribers, reversing a negative trend, over the last couple of months was directly attributable to Sean and his groundbreaking reporting.

When Julian told Tibbets that he could not comment on advice of his counsel, the young Tibbets dropped his shoulder and pressed on. When Julian responded for the tenth time that he had no comment, he thought Tibbets was going to physically accost him and was satisfied to note that this skinny kid was no threat to the newly Mannified physique of Julian Dickerson.

"Poor kid," he thought as Tibbets left in a huff with a precarious grip of his various reporter's accoutrements.

"Careful there, kid. Hey, I'll tell you what. My codefendant Lois Coronetti Carson might have a little more to say on the subject. You should be able to track her down at Barcus Bar and Grill."

"Barcus Bar and Grill?"

"Yeah, Mitch's."

"Oh, Mitch's. Thanks, Mr. Dickerson. Thanks, an awful lot."

Julian couldn't wait to tell someone about the trick he pulled on Lois. Unfortunately, no matter how he explained it, Manny failed to see the humor. Julian consoled himself that Manny didn't seem to see the humor in anything. His fearless taskmaster was just a straight up serious guy and Julian could not fault him for this. His passion and those he hoped to share it with more than made up for it.

"I'll call Mitch after my workout," Julian thought to himself.

'He's gonna love this."

As it turned out, not only did Mitch love the little prank and delight in witnessing Lois going toe to toe with Tibbets, he managed to offer the kid a beer and get him to write a vanity piece about the joint.

"It's a win, win," Jules and Mitch agreed.

"Gonna put this place on the map, Julian. Gonna put it on the map."

CHAPTER
Six

Mitch's prediction was more on target than anyone could have expected. The feel-good story was picked up by the Associated Press and rose to the surface in a sea of sad, tragic, scary, and unpleasant news. The Chamber of Commerce insisted on giving Barcus Bar and Grill a prominent spot on the town website and Travelocity soon featured several multi-star reviews.

Suddenly, the bar was famous and Barcus was famous. This resulted in a significant uptick in business, which weighed heavily on the kitchen staff, Lois. She threatened to quit until the publicity frenzy was usurped by a story about a waterfall in the next town over where an elderly gentleman had seen a vision of the Blessed Virgin Mary, which he was able to capture, kind of, sort of, on his flip phone camera.

By the time Lois was able to get away and visit Julian, she asserted right from the outset that the onslaught had been all his fault. That Mitch had told her everything. After accepting Julian's forced apology, she had to admit there was some consolation in the fact that they had taken in a shit ton of money and now had the funds to buy a new fridge and finish one of the bathrooms in Mitch's unfinished house.

Soon after this, the various medical experts, like a bunch of wizards of Oz, finally decreed from behind their veil of inscrutable prognostications and medi-babble that Julian was sufficiently ambulatory to get the hell out of the hospital.

He was beyond joyous for his release back into the general population, but couldn't have predicted, not for one minute, the welcome home surprise bash that awaited him at Barcus Bar and Grill. The joint's new namesake was the first to greet him as he hobbled in the door and then fell back out again with the force of his big boy's loyalty and affection. Lois to the rescue lifted her friend up off the gravel and carried him back in. He felt a little like a Muppet with his legs dangling limply over her forearm, but the many happy faces that greeted him like a sky full of balloons made him forget the less than dignified reentry.

Mitch was in good form, serving up pitchers full of his famous poor man's punch. No one enjoyed these more than Mrs. Stuart it seemed, and Lois would eventually be enlisted to transport the fine lady out of the bar similarly to how she'd gotten Julian in. Neither was Julian moderate in his consumption. Life was good. He had so many friends. Mitch, Lois, Lois's ex-husband and their daughter Shelley, Mrs. Stuart, Manny, Snodgrass the lawyer, Tirana, Tirana's ex-husband, even cub reporter Sean Tibbets escorting none other than Donna C.

"Hey there, Mr. D," she said brightly while pulling him in for a this side, no that side, no this side kiss on the cheek.

"Hey, you look like a thousand dollars or maybe it's more dollars. Anyways, you look like however many dollars it is."

"I think you mean bucks," Sean offered.

"Bucks? What are you talking about? Don't mind, Sean, Mr. D. You know these reporter types, always correcting everyone's grammatical appropriateness. He might be cute, but we think he should keep his journalistic tendencies to himself. Am I right?"

Donna then gave Julian and Sean the wink of all winks. A wink that seemed to last for several minutes. A length of a wink that was so distracting that it wiped most of the previous commentary out of mind and replaced it with immediate concern that the winker might never be able to unwink her wink.

But unwink Donna did just before Lois was about to slap her in the face. Donna observed the puzzled expressions on those surrounding her.

"You guys," she said with a chortle. "Stop staring at me. I can't help it if I'm a long winker. Is that it? My dad says I'm a super long winker. I guess that's just me. Honest to gosh, I think people don't wink long enough or at least most of them. Then, people are like was that a wink or did the person just get something in their eye. If I wink, you will always know it's a wink."

No one in the group could really argue with Donna's logic or at least none of them was willing to try. Sean just beamed easily, giving himself away as a young man in love.

"God bless his soul," Lois whispered to Tirana.

"Amen to that, Lo."

Manny entertained the crowd with standing backflips. Mitch took them on a tour of the new fridge. Snodgrass sat in a booth on his phone for most of the afternoon. Lois and Tirana's exes talked politics and football and at the behest of Mrs. Stuart, who seemed to be flirting with them, briefly touched on the fact that they both had been married to lesbians.

"She was the one who seduced me," Tirana's ex protested.

"Me too. Lois called the shots. I had nuthin to do with it."

"It happens," Mrs. Stuart offered from her professional perspective, albeit a slightly inebriated one.

"I used to run across it every now and again and I always told my clients the best cure for a broken heterosexual heart is to try to find that trust again. Most of us women are not lesbians, only ten percent if I remember correctly. Me, I've never been attracted to a woman in that way, not ever, I'm strictly a man lover, if you know what I mean."

"Ahh, good, that's good. You married? asked Tirana's ex.

"Not since husband number three kicked the bucket," Mrs. Stuart said and added with a coy little curtsey, "I'm a free woman."

At this, both men shuffled awkwardly, backed away just perceptibly and had their attention drawn to the ceiling and their shoes intermittently.

"Can somebody get a lady a drink?" Stuart asked.

As the two practically fell over one another in service of her request, she felt encouraged. When neither returned and she was required to get a drink for herself, she drank it down sufficiently quickly to forget the entire interlude.

Out of the corner of her eye, she spotted Manny doing a headstand, his tee shirt puddling around his neck and armpits and his six pack exposed for the world to see. She wondered how in God's name she had failed to notice her coworker's many good qualities and was determined to get to know him a whole lot better and fast.

This imagined love connection did eventually manifest, but ended about as quickly as Manny could do a backflip and land on his feet. Clarissa Stuart had not worn a pair of yoga pants ever in her life and she wasn't about to start now. Manny's standards could therefore not be met and besides she couldn't stomach the taste or even the smell of protein shakes.

"Life is too short, Manny," she would later tell him. "You're all about the gym and I'm more of a nature walk kind of girl."

Knowing he still did and always would retain his first love, himself, Manny took it all very well.

Clarissa was later to discover, as if a blind person gaining sight, that the man of her dreams, her forever soul mate had been right in front of her the whole time. She'd been so busy chasing after riff-raff that she'd skipped right over the gentle Mitch who turned out to be everything she had ever wanted. She would make it her business to tell him so.

Meanwhile, at Julian's surprise party, Donna and Sean and Lois's daughter, Shelley, formed their own little young people's cadre. They broke into fits of laughter with increasing frequency as if their ginger ales were more potent than any cocktail. Julian was happy to see that Shelley was in good form, and, when he apologized for having missed her Prom, she assured him it was nice to think that she even had a date and that, of course, she understood.

"Thanks, Shelley," Julian responded. "Say, how was your graduation?"

"Well it didn't exactly happen. I missed too much school due to having one of my bouts."

"I'm really, really sorry to hear that."

"It's okay. Dad and I decided I could just go for a GED."

'I'm sure that'll work out just fine, a smart kid like you."

"If you can still call a twenty-two year old a kid," Shelley joked.

"You do have a point there," Julian replied as he found himself appraising Shelley in a new light.

After a detailed conversation about their lawsuit with Snodgrass that only he was sober enough to remember, Lois left Julian to join Tirana in the kitchen. The guests were soon treated to a beef chili that Julian declared was the best thing he had ever eaten, ever!

The festivities culminated in Julian's attempt at a headstand that was not quite as successful as Manny's. Mrs. Stuart couldn't help but observe this with a touch of unprofessional disdain.

"And to imagine I ever had feelings for this guy," She thought as Manny showed up with her ninth and final refill of Mitch's delicious punch.

Donna regretted that the three-hour drive back to her parent's house necessitated her departure.

"Wait, you have a license now?" Julian asked.

"Well, not technically speaking if you catch what I mean. See, daddy thought since mother is not safe to go behind the wheel of anything, much less a moving car that could kill somebody in an accident, he decided that I should have her license. This was right after she parked the Escalade half in the garage and half in the laundry room. He calls it 'taking matters into our own hands.'"

"Hmmm. Okay, but what happens if you get pulled over?"

"Nothing."

"Nothing? You sure about that?"

"Yes, I'm sure and you want to know why I'm sure? Because I was already pulled over like three times, once by the same officer. But look at me, Mr. D, I mean seriously, would you give a ticket violation to such a young and innocent girl if you pulled me over and you were a police? I don't think so. And while we're at it, how come, I've been wanting to ask, did I not receive a letter or even a note after sending you a long, nice letter back from you? Or even a text message would have been good enough."

"Sorry about that, Donna. I was going through a lot. Your letter was very much appreciated."

"Okay, I'll accept, if you can promise me one thing."

"What's that?"

"What's what?"

"What's the one thing?"

"Oh that! It's a letter, Mr. D, a letter or even just a note."

"Consider it done."

"You mean you already wrote it to me."

"No, but I intend to."

"Well, don't be acting like it's done until you actually do it, okay?"

"OK."

Julian awoke the next morning feeling uncharacteristically optimistic. He hadn't dreamt about pole vaulting, but he felt like he had. The insult of hitting his head on the underside of the table as he sat up from his berth in the corner booth at Mitch's Barcus Bar and Grill was fleeting. The small knot that was forming on his crown was sore to the touch in an oddly irresistible way. He wasn't in the hospital, not anymore. All of his friends had been there to celebrate his release, him the pole vaulter, the man among men.

He yawned, stretched out his arms, tensed his biceps and arghhed like a pirate. Barcus sprang up from the floor below and licked his face. Someone stirred in the booth next door and as it's massive form ascended into view, Julian instantly regained a sense of his tininess and vulnerability.

"Shut the fuck up," the creature called out and Julian recognized the semi-baritone voice of his friend Lois; that and her signature form of expression.

"Oh, hey, Lo. What the hell are you doing here?"

"It's complicated, Buddy. Lemme start the coffee up. That urn of Mitch's takes for frigging ever and this fair lady could drink about a gallon of it about now."

Julian and Lois parted ways at the respective thresholds of the Guys and the Dolls. The concept of unisex bathrooms had not yet arrived in the mental lexicon of Mitchell Mitch O'Gorman and probably never would.

After a quick coldwater splash bath at the sink and other ablutions common to civilized man, Julian, excited, felt like the million bucks Donna had meant to ascribe to his appearance the day before. He looked out the bay window and saw Barcus bounding after a tennis ball, each time dutifully returning it to Mitch. He experienced a twinge of jealousy, but just a twinge, and headed out to join in the game of fetch.

"After all," he thought. "When was the last time I played fetch? And just the fact that I have the option is its own miracle."

Once the boys had thoroughly worn themselves out and Julian was beginning to feel the knee just a bit, they came back inside. Lois had set the giant urn on the bar. Julian heard the last steamy gasp of percolation and caught the aroma of Dunkin Donuts breakfast blend. He hadn't had a good cup of Joe, come to think of it, in quite some time either.

The three sat shoulder to shoulder facing the bar and sipped on their hot mugs of dark, dark coffee in silence like dialysis patients waiting for the life-saving liquid to deliver itself through their veins.

When Barcus trotted over and scratched on Mitch's leg, Mitch got up and went around the bar. Like magic, he produced a large bowl of kibble over which he sprinkled a handful of beer nuts. Lois went back to the kitchen and came back with a package of Little Debbie cinnamon buns for the boys and toast piled high with cottage cheese for herself.

Julian offered her a Debbie, but she waved her hand at the thing and with a mouthful of her breakfast of choice explained, "I'm on a diet."

"Starting when?" Julian asked as he looked her up and down for any sign of this.

"Starting now," she said.

"What does that make it? Six or seven diets you started up in the last two months?" Mitch asked as he fed his lanky frame with a third cake.

"Mind your own business, Mitch," Lois said as she eyed her empty plate and then fixated on the last remaining cinnamon bun.

"Anybody eating that?" she asked.

As the two men sat dumbfounded at Lois's ability to eat a not small cinnamon bun in two bites, she was licking the icing off each finger one at a time.

"Delicious," she said and, as she looked up, "What are you two staring at? Never saw a gorgeous woman having a nibble before?"

Neither Julian nor Mitch could come up with a response other than to try to look like they hadn't heard the question.

Lois let out a satisfied belch.

"We need to talk business, Gentlemen. Jules, you asked me earlier what I was doing sleeping in the booth last night; well, it wasn't 'cause I was worried about getting a DUI. You know how I can hold my liquor. No, I was sleeping in the booth because that is where I've been sleeping for the past six weeks. Except when Tirana doesn't have the boys. She's got two teenage boys."

"Nice kids?"

"Super nice, but stay with me, this is important. Why have I been sleeping in the booth, you'll be wondering; well, Mitch knows and Tirana knows and now you're about to know, course I didn't want to bring it up until you were out of the hospital."

"Bring up what, Lois? Go on, you're scaring me."

"You scare far too easy, my friend, but that's a whole other subject, or, wait a minute, maybe it's not another subject. I was worried you would freak out so please try not to. I rented out my place."

"You did what?"

"I rented out my place and I'm living here at Mitch's for free. And you want to know why I rented my place, Julian? I rented it because lawyers are expensive and we, you and me, needed a lawyer."

"What about contingency? I thought you told me, Snodgrass had so much faith in our case, he was doing it on contingency."

"Yes, I did tell you that, Julian, but it was only half true because Snodgrass is only half doing it on contingency, the other half had to be paid as you go."

"So, you're living here?"

"Just until we can afford to put heat, flooring and a staircase in Mitch's house. Oh, and plumbing and sheetrock. It's really not that bad here in the booth though, my friend. Of course, I don't experience the luxury of having room to stretch out my legs unlike some people I know."

"Very funny, but geez, Lois, what the hell? Have you lost your mind?"

"Maybe I have, Jules, but you're gonna be thanking your lucky stars that I did because we are going to be rich. And all I'm asking from you is to pitch in your little bit of savings. Mitch here has done his part already."

"What's in it for Mitch?"

"Well, you dissolve your IRS or whatever it is and hand it over and I take out a loan against my house, which, by the way, is fully paid for, and we use half of the money for the lawyer and the other half to settle Mitch's taxes and finish up his unfinished house and then we all get to live there. Mitch gets us to pitch in here at his place for free, help him turn things around and we each get a third interest in the business and another third interest in a brand new house. We win the lawsuit, Mitch gets his cut of the pot."

"That makes no sense, Lois. What happens if we lose? Everyone gets nothing?"

"We lose, we have a bar to fall back on. Haven't you always wanted to own a bar, Jules? And a house, a nicer house than the one you shared with that bitch from hell, and hey, you can't beat the commute."

"No, Lois, I can't honestly say I've ever even thought about owning a bar. I was planning on using my savings to get a place to live for me and Barcus and buy a used Toyota."

"Yeah, I thought you'd say that, but you've got to start thinking a little bigger, my friend, I mean like new Ferrari bigger. Meanwhile, though, you won't be needing a car and Barcus and you are going to live here with us. And as for work, there's plenty to go around, Mitch has you covered."

"Covered doing what?"

"Well not teaching English Lit, that's for damn sure. I mean real work. Roll up your sleeves and get shit done kind of work."

"What, like washing dishes? Is that the bright future you have in mind for me?"

"Nothing wrong with washing dishes, little man. Hey, and maybe we can get you a pair of those stilt things like the clowns walk around on."

"And that would be for what?" Julian's mouth enunciated from the lower quadrant of his alarmingly red face.

"So you could tend the bar and actually be able to see your customers," Lois slapped Julian on the back and doubled over in appreciation of her own wit.

"Very funny," Julian said and climbed down off his barstool.

"Where you going?" Mitch managed to spit out between belly laughs.

"Going for a walk. Taking Barcus. I don't know where we're going, just not here."

"Calm down, little fella, just pulling your leg, er making a little joke, ahh, I mean having some fun with you," Lois protested.

"Whatever," Julian said. "C'mon boy."

All of Julian's savings didn't amount to very much after all, but it would have covered a cozy studio over Wax and Wayne, a candle shop in town cleverly incorporating it's proprietor's given name.

When this very Wayne turned out to be a lonely and long winded fellow looking more for a best friend than a tenant and took over an hour to point out the important features of the one room and suggested that Barcus was welcome to live out in the yard, Julian thought better of it. Nothing else being available in his price range and the pressure from Lois to contribute to the cause getting more intense by the day, he tried to put a positive spin on being his pushy pal's boothmate.

A significant consolidator of that tenuous spin was to get Mitch and Lois to agree to convert half of the overly large pantry into a kind of mother-in-law's apartment until the house had the basic amenities of heat and running water. Manny, who was strong as hell and handy with a hammer, was enlisted as head contractor, and Tirana took Lois thrifting to furnish and prettify the featureless box inexpensively but to pleasant effect. Within two weeks, Julian was excited to move out of the booth and into the relative luxury of his and Lois' new pad. But this was not to be since Lois had taken the opportunity to invite Tirana to stay over with her for a change.

"I always stay at her place, Julie. And without, Tirana, there'd be no curtains on the windows,"

"There are no windows, Lois."

"Well, sue me for speaking euphemistically or whatever. You know what I mean."

"Metaphorically."

"Yes, that's right, Mr. English literature, as metaphorically as you like."

For any number of reasons, none of which were fear-based, Julian would assert, he demurred. Lois did have a point about how helpful Tirana had been and she saved him and Lois and Mitch from a diet of Pop Tarts and frozen pizza as often as she possibly could. Her incredible chili would be made in sufficient quantities to cover their needs and those of their patrons a week per batch. Of this manna, Julian could never get enough. In addition, Tirana was just so damn nice. So nice that she even seemed to bring out a certain niceness in Lois that Julian had never witnessed or experienced before. When she was around, Julie felt not only mothered, but kind of double mothered. Anyway, the booth was not so bad as all that and had become quite tolerable since he managed to remember now, upon awakening, that there was a tabletop within inches of his head.

In addition to all this, Julian was quite dependent on Lois as transportation was distinctly unavailable to him in her absence. Mitch still rode his electric bike as weather permitted, even though he'd long since gotten his license back.

"What can I tell you, I like it. Cars are so confining and the price of gas? Holy geez. I'd go broke just on the price of gas all by itself."

Julian knew that it was really more about Mitch being a creature of habit than of being thrifty. Even if there were a bus route along this two lane highway that bridged one washed up New England town to another in a county that had more cows than people, Mitch would take his bike.

Julian needed Lois to be his chauffeur and, though she didn't actually charge him, this service did come with a price. So he and Barcus curled up in their booth for one last night, or as it turned out, two, while Lois and her love test drove the new room.

His coffers having been revitalized with Julian's remaining nest egg, Snodgrass prepared to depose a long list of witnesses, beginning with Fitz and stretching as far as 'My Name is

Chessie' from the Best Western College Park Inn, whom he would later classify as 'reluctant.'

Julian took to tending the bar like a natural and found that he actually enjoyed it. Life was good. He was out of the hospital, among friends, no longer navigating a hostile wife and an ugly divorce. He found as the weeks wore on that there was really nothing at all about his old life that he missed, apart from a less demanding left knee.

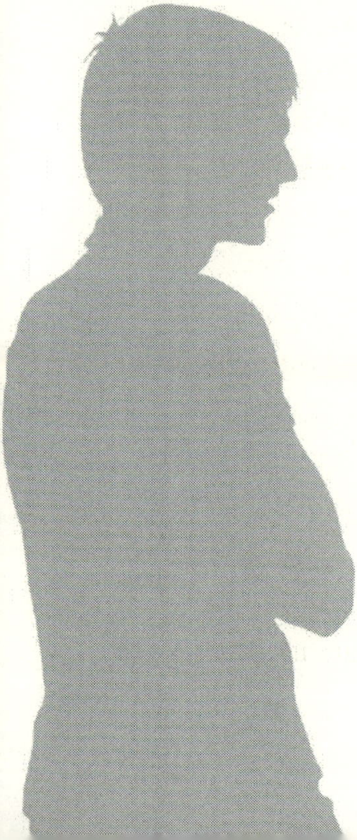

CHAPTER
Seven

Doreen O'Gorman nee Kaliboski disembarked as gingerly as possible from the high step of the Greyhound Dreamliner into the bus terminal of a New England town she never guessed would reclaim her. Among her valuables, secured in a straw tote bag colorfully embroidered with cacti and the words 'Vegas or Bust,' was a jumbo package of gum with but one remaining stick, a curling iron, a Hollywood change purse, several salted peanuts floating around lose at the bottom with hairpins and sticky bits of dried pineapple, a bus schedule, a People Magazine from sometime in the previous decade and a newspaper unfamiliar to these parts.

She wore a wrinkled sundress that did nothing for her petite and curvaceous figure, but definitely spoke to a long hard journey. Her white high heels were quite badly scuffed and incongruous with her otherwise casual attire as if a bride had changed out of everything but the shoes.

She easily identified her maroon American Tourister from the belly of the bus. The pink ribbon tied to its handle was tattered, but the case itself had only a few signs of wear. She loved that bag. It was a good looking bag, for sure, but, more importantly, it had those wheels. She repossessed it with pride and engaged the pull along feature despite the fact that she was hauling about five pounds worth of empty luggage. To say she had lost everything was accurate; everything.

How she managed to rock up to Mitch's Barcus Bar and Grill is a story unto itself. But suffice it to say, rock up she did. Her first and only cordial greeting was from the dog who sniffed intently at the bottom of her straw tote. Then, Lois appeared.

"Lois? What the fuck are you doin here?"

"What am I doing here, Doreen? What am I doing here? I happen to live here. Yeah, that's right, I live here now and you obviously do not."

"Well, we'll just see about who lives where, Lois. What did my husband go gay or something? Get himself a big Lesbo of a girlfriend?"

"Watch your mouth, sweetheart, and leave your attitude at the door. In fact, you can leave your entire self at the door and turn around and go back to the armpit you crawled out of. And anyway, where's the house? How is it you show up here without the house?"

The front door swung open and tall, lanky Mitch appeared and disappeared just as quickly back into the shadow of the room. He then proceeded to come forward timidly like a man about to face his maker.

"Doreen? What the hell? Doreen? Is that you?"

"Mitchy!" Doreen called out in her best babydoll voice. "Mitchy, Mitchy, Mitchy."

As Doreen threw open her arms and ran toward her husband, navigating the gravel with her high heels the best she could, Lois interceded with a full frontal body block.

"You think you can just come waltzing back in here after what you did to this good and decent man? You broke this good man's damn heart, bitch. And what the hell did you do with his fucking house that you and your boyfriend ran off with? Where's the house, Doreen?"

"Mitchy, you gonna let this big ol diesel dyke keep me from comin' here with my head between my knees feeling so sorry and wanting just to apologize with all my heart and make it up to my number one man?"

"Well, hey now, Doreen. Easy, easy. Lois here is my good friend. She is just trying to help. No need for the name calling. Why don't we take this inside and have a nice grown up conversation about it?"

"She's not coming in here without the house, Mitch. We need to know what the hell she's done with your house and why she thinks she can just show up here without it."

"Urgggh. I'm gonna count to ten, Mitch. I'm gonna close my eyes and count to ten and when I open my eyes I swear to God, this one better be outta my way. I'm here to claim my rightful share of your famous establishment that I read about even in a diner in Vegas. A diner in Vegas and there it was."

Doreen grabbed the newspaper out of her tote as though presenting Exhibit A.

Lois went to wrestle the paper out of her hand and a cat fight to end all cat fights ensued. Mitch tried to intervene, but needed to call Julian for back up. The girls rolled around in the parking lot, kicking up clouds of dust through which hair grabbing, scratching and even biting could be observed intermittently. Even with Julian's help, the men were utterly ineffectual. If Lois hadn't landed on Doreen's prized suitcase and thereby crushed and destroyed it, who knows if anyone would have come out alive.

"You fucking bitch. Now look what you've done," Doreen said while staggering backwards into the waiting arms of her husband who held her tightly as she melted into a cascade of self-pitying tears.

Soon after, the four could be found sitting in a booth. Lois uncharacteristically nursed a beer as Doreen sipped at a pina colada and held a bar towel filled with ice up to her left eye.

"That snake took me for everything I was worth. He comes along like Don fuckin Juan and here I'm feeling so not loved by my own husband who just wants to work and work and work all the time, and promised me, promised me a real house, not on wheels, and what does he give me? The same old house on wheels and a beautiful new house, a real house that never gets finished so we can move into it. Up till a couple minutes ago, I had an American Tourister suitcase on wheels, but I didn't want my house to be on wheels. So I took the damn house and we went to Vegas and my so-called boyfriend who was gonna show me the good life, you know, the razzle and dazzle, turns out to be a bad gambler. And I'm working the night shift at a roadstop because he forgot to tell me that no one wants to hire a show girl who don't know how to sing besides dancing and I can't sing worth a damn, or so I'm told. So, the house you're all worried about, the piece of crap house, Lois, you can go get it off of the guy who won it from my ex in a game of five card stud. Good luck with that. Piece of shit."

At this, Lois jumped up out of her seat opposite Doreen and went for her jugular.

"Who you calling a piece of shit?"

"No, hold off. I wasn't saying it about you. I was saying it about my ex or maybe even the trailer, but not about you, Lois."

"Okay, okay, but watch yourself, Doreen. So, why exactly are you here and what is it you want from Mitch?"

"Well, I've never been much for religion, but I do know one thing they say in the Bible."

"And what exactly is that?"

"That, Lois, is that you're supposed to forgive us trespassers just like Jesus would have done. And that is why I was hoping that Mitch, being as how he went to Catholic school and all, would find it in his dear big heart to forgive lil ol' me. Can you Mitchy-poo? Can you forgive your naughty, naughty little girl who is so so sowwy?"

Julian and Lois watched Mitch cave before their eyes.

"Oh, no you don't, Mitch. Mitch, Mitch, look at me. It's your friend Lois talking."

Mitch held up his bony piano player hand and spoke for himself for a change.

"Look, Lo, I know you got my back and I really, really appreciate that, my friend. But Doreen here, maybe if she wasn't so damn teensy and fragile like, geez, I don't know, I think she has a point there about the Bible and all, and it's a fact that I did go to Catholic school. I went to Catholic school all the way through my senior year and what am I gonna do now? Ignore everything that they taught us there? Turn the other cheek and all?"

"Well, don't blame us if she hauls back and slaps you silly on that other cheek, Mitch, like she did the first one. But it's your life, pal."

"Yes, Mitch, you have to listen to your heart, after all. And God knows we could use an extra hand around here," Julian offered.

At this, Lois jabbed Julian hard in the gut and he decided to leave it be. Barcus put his big head in his master's lap with his usual perfect timing.

Both Julian and Lois achieved the fairly obvious conclusion that Mitch was responding to his wife with a tinge of Catholic guilt. Smartly considering that it probably wasn't the best time, no one hastened to volunteer that Mitch had recently formed a romantic attachment with Clarissa Stuart and they were pretty hot and heavy.

It had all started rather coyly when Mitch accepted Clarissa's invitation to be her test case in her attempt to get certified for Dr. Broadkind's Do A Better You life coaching system. Both therapist and patient were thrilled to mark great progress, but not so thrilled as they were to experience the ecstasy of jumping into Mitch's bed together. Dr. Broadkind fell by the wayside, but Mitch and Clarissa would forever be grateful for how his system changed their lives.

Julian was happy for them. He was happy for Lois and Tirana. Overall, this new life, far from the stifling rigidity of academia and his foregone mission to influence young minds in direct competition with a potpourri of recreational drugs, raging hormones and considerable other distractions, was deeply gratifying. Nonetheless, he had to admit to a loneliness that seemed to only be exacerbated by his closest friends' romantic good fortunes. He had his dog and a rewarding sense of his contribution to the success of the bar. But he found that even the unwanted flirtation of his erstwhile smitten student Donna had ceased with her newfound interest in Sean Tibbets, cub reporter, and wondered if it was possible to feel nostalgic for unwanted attention. He suspected so.

The lawsuit was a good distraction, but that only went so far. Long hikes with Barcus cleared his lungs of the musky beer and tobacco atmosphere of Mitch's and freed him of Lois's constant, albeit good natured, badgering. As he contemplated his own solitude, he couldn't help noticing that he actually felt sympathy for Doreen as well. Here she was, thinking that all would be forgiven, which it would (Mitch was that kind hearted) and that she and the man she was still legally married to would renew their partnership on an intimate level, which they would not. Though she didn't know it yet, she and Julian were pretty much in the same boat. The odd men out. Sometimes, it occurred to Julian that he was sick of being the odd man out; the guy who never had to duck for cover because he was already preset at ducking height and the crossfire pretty much flew right over his head. Maybe this was it. Just him and his dog and his work at the bar and the lawsuit for as long as that lasted.

"Some pole vaulter," he thought.

Meanwhile, it was impossible to ignore the fact that with love came complications. Julian watched his friend Mitch going through this big time. He was thrashed and twisted between his love and lust for Clarissa and his sense of loyalty to the little woman he had vowed to stand by through thick and thin and had sworn to before the eyes of God.

Lois made it quite clear where she stood on the matter and rapidly traded in her nonchalance with regard to Clarissa to a fierce female warrior allegiance. As far as she was concerned, Doreen had stepped all over those vows she and Mitch had made, and they were no longer worth the paper they were memorialized on.

"You have more grounds for divorce than a raisin has wrinkles. And, think about it, Mitch, you gonna throw a good woman like Clarissa to the curb because your cheating ex-wife crawled out of the gutter when she got a whiff that you might be banking a little cash for once? Can't you see what she's trying to pull here?"

"I know, Lo. I hear ya. It's just that I took the vows. I took the vows and I can't just untake them."

"It's called a divorce, Mitch. Happens all the time."

Jules steered clear of this particular debate. On one hand, he completely agreed with Lois, but, on the other, he had to admire Mitch's integrity and he couldn't deny feeling a tad bit of sympathy for Doreen. After all, it's not like she had it easy in life and he knew this as she had shared with him the travails of her escape to Vegas and also how closely the experience was reminiscent of a transient childhood. She really was trailer trash, he discovered, but that was no more her choice than his lack of height was his. Maybe if Mitch had actually made the effort to settle his young wife in a house with a foundation...

Doreen's contribution to the business turned out to be detectable, but just barely, until Mitch could be convinced that her skills as a waitress did not extend beyond the condiment station and it was best she stay out of the kitchen altogether. Mitch's awakening on this score occurred one morning when Doreen held up a steaming hot piece of toast that looked like a relic from Chernobyl and insisted that it was simply well done and perfectly good.

Lois suggested that she eat it herself, adding "You're the one who loves toast so much."

"Well, why don't you pass me the jam and butter and I'll do just that, Lois!"

"Here you go, princess. I'll pay good money to see this shit show."

After slathering the toast with I Can't Believe It's Not Butter and a daub of Smuckers strawberry jam, Doreen proceeded to munch with a vengeance. Her full-mouth display of culinary satisfaction revealed a black hole that made her appear toothless. She gave a big, unsettling smile, then faked a fulsome swallow, brought her napkin to her mouth and spit the ball of ash into it.

Lois wasn't buying this act and demanded that the napkin be handed over for examination.

"What are you, the food police? I don't think anyone would hire you as the food police, Lois. And you know why they wouldn't? Because you'd eat all the evidence, that's why."

"Very clever, Doreen. You got comic skills to match your toast making skills. Maybe if you can't make it as a showgirl in Vegas you could go back there and be a stand-up comedian."

"I could do it better than some lesbians I know. What would you do, Lois, tell a bunch of lesbian jokes? That'd go over like a lead balloon."

"You ignorant piece of trash that even a trailer wouldn't accept. And speaking of trailers, why don't you just go back to Vegas and be a famous comic who's not funny or a showgirl who can't sing or a diner waitress who can't make a piece of toast or just do what I bet you really might be able to handle for cash and buy back Mitch's trailer that you stole."

"Who you calling a thief?"

Lois looked around the empty bar room and glanced outside where Mitch and Julian and Barcus were playing an innocent game of Frisbee and enjoying the first hint of Autumn.

"Ahhh, I guess that must be you, Doreen. Since I'm the only other person here and you are and I'm not."

The boys stumbled in the front door and just caught this last statement of fact.

Mitch sniffed the air and tried to change the subject.

"Something burning in here?"

"The only thing burning is little old Doreen, Mitchy, because Lois here is making false accusations."

"Well, geez, Honeybunch, don't look at me. I didn't say nuthin about the incident at Holly Hobby."

"What incident at Holly Hobby?" Julian and Lois asked in unison.

"Oh, never mind. It ain't important and it was so not my fault, so you don't trouble yourselves over it, alright?"

"What incident at Holly Hobby, Mitch?"

"Geez, sometimes, I really need to learn to keep my big mouth shut."

"You can say that again, Mitchums."

"Ok, you're not gonna come clean? Lemme guess, this must have happened during Doreen's glue phase."

"No, Lois, no it did not. It was a self-improvement project and yes, I needed glue, but not to sniff it like you so evilly think, but to do my Vision Board of what direction I wanted my life to go. But this is what I get for my trouble of trying to better myself. I get a petty larceny and a dyke like you trying to call me a criminal. And look who's talking when I have come to be informed that you and your teeny-weeny sidekick here who can't barely see over the bar have acquired part ownership of my husband's business that we struggled for so many years for and you two just waltz in. Talk about a thief!"

Mitch, who hated confrontation and was normally a man of few words grabbed a bar rag, wiped his brow and prepared to take control of the situation.

"Now, now" he said. "Let's everybody just pipe down and try to get along with each other. We have many things to be thankful for. We have a growing business, which would not have been possible without Lois and Julian AND Barcus here. You, Doreen, have magically appeared back in my life like a little fairy princess and my lonely days and days of financial stress appear to be over. Now, none of us, not one, with maybe the exception of Barcus and Julian and maybe me, which kind of leaves you two ladies, but really mostly Doreen, has not made some pretty major mistakes, but that is all behind us. We get to start again with a fresh slate and make a new and better life for ourselves. We need to thank God for His mercy and we need to try to be a little more cooperative with one another. After all, we're kind of all the family we've got."

The audience of three sat in stunned silence. None of them had ever heard Mitch say so many words in a row. It really was a case in which quantity was easily as impactful as quality. They might all be sitting there still if Barcus hadn't drawn their attention by nuzzling open the napkin he'd managed to pull off Doreen's lap and consuming a glob of pre-chewed burnt toast like it was the most desirable delicacy on God's green earth.

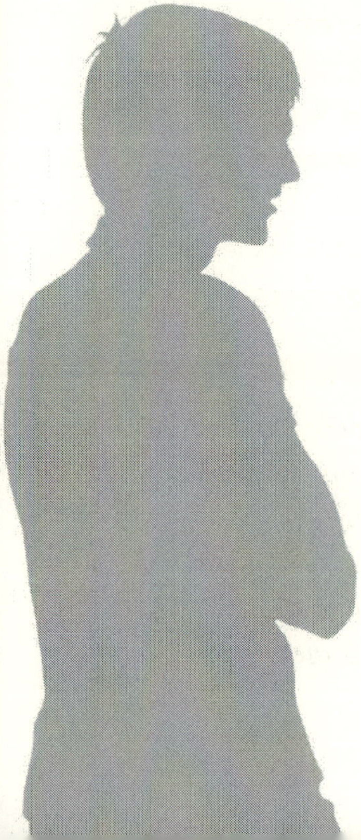

CHAPTER
Eight

As a courtesy to Mitch and in an effort to restore the smooth-running atmosphere of Barcus Bar and Grill, Lois agreed to try, just try, to go a little easier on Doreen. This helped a bit, but not as much as arranging to have their shifts place them as physically distant from one another as possible. Tirana, when she was available, tried to offer a kindly buffer between the two and had just enough charm to pull it off.

Julian, as was his custom, steered clear of controversy, especially when it involved two highly entitled females who were willing to go to the mat to establish dominance. When he wasn't managing the weekly orders or balancing the books, he kept himself busy as the world's least conspicuous busboy and worked the service bar from a platform he and Mitch had devised out of empty wine crates. Julian loved the appearance of height this afforded and wished dearly that it was more than just the appearance. On more occasions than one, upon chatting up a promising romantic prospect from his lofty perch, he had at some point needed to descend and thereby reveal his actual stature. This was more than humiliating, but the brief thrill of a possible love connection kept him coming back for more.

Opportunities for these encounters increased with the popularity of the place. Business was booming. Even Doreen proved something of a magnet for a certain element who could park their semis in Mitch's big lot, enjoy a late supper knowing that Mitch would sneak them in after the 2 a.m. state limit all while enjoying Doreen's flirtations. They slept in their cabs right there and could be on hand for an early breakfast too.

Meanwhile, the sleeping arrangements for the staff and co-owners of Barcus Bar and Grill had improved greatly with the near completion of Mitch's house. Julian, at last, had a room of his own, though it doubled as the kitchen. As soon as they had a staircase, he and Barcus would be set.

As Snodgrass continued to ply their lawsuit, Julian and Lois began to realize that their dreams of fortune might be materializing without benefit of a big win in court. That is, if Snodgrass wasn't so damned expensive.

"What's that, Lo? Don't tell me, another bill from Snodgrass."

Julian sipped his beer and placed an UNO card down on the pile. Lois waved the envelope she'd just opened and tossed it over to her friend.

"Holy shit, another three grand? What the hell? How much is it going to cost us to actually go to court? This is ridiculous."

"Pipe down, Jules. No one said that going up against the man was ever going to be cheap or easy. We're at war. This is an actual war, Julian, and you've gotta stay tough. You've gotta stay focused."

"What I'm focused on, Lo, is this bill and the fifty other bills like it that we already have paid and the fifty more to come. I say, we settle or we're going to end up spending all the money we're making here with Mitch on making Snodgrass rich."

"Snodgrass fees will be peanuts compared to what we stand to get if he does his job right."

"And how do we know if he's doing that? We're not lawyers. He could be playing us, Lo. For god's sake, he could be in Fitzgerald's pocket all this time, double dipping and keeping the wealthiest family in town on his good side. Think about it."

"Well, now, Mister conspiracy theory, how about we don't go making up chicken shit stories about being double-crossed? You think Snodgrass would even think about it? Look at who he'd have to answer to, Jules? He'd have to answer to this."

Lois tensed her arm to reveal a bicep formidable enough to emerge from her beefy arm.

She threw down a card and said, "UNO." And that was the end of that conversation.

Julian thought about how he resented that Lois always had the last word. But also, on this occasion, he dearly hoped her last word was right.

Fitz Prep managed to reopen in the Fall despite the legal challenges it faced on several fronts. Donna C. was among the 30% of the previous year's student body who returned, bus accidents, notwithstanding. She and young Tibbets remained a thing and Barcus Bar was their rendezvous.

Donna was thrilled to reconnect with her old role models and to fill them in on the losers who had taken their places as PE teacher and English Lit. teacher respectively.

"Who ever heard of a Phys-ed teacher whose specialty is yoga, Lois? (Now that you've said it's A-okay for me to call you that.) Isn't yoga for people who are foreigners not from here? And are we supposed to think it's a sport? What happened to volleyball? I can't stretch like that, and if I even really want to, I am so not sure if I could."

"I feel you, kid. What the hell is this country coming to? Diversity, dismercity, I say. Lemme have a bunch of kids and a ball and a net without mouse holes in it and a drive to win; win at any cost, now that's what I call America."

Lois, who still wasn't used to not having a whistle around her neck, made as if to put one to her lips and mouthed a 'toot' toot.'

"High five, Miss Lois, I mean Lois."

Donna offered her upraised hand and completely missed her approach to that of her former gym teacher.

"Ooops, sorry."

"No worries, kid. Hand-eye was never really your thing. It's all good."

"Who are you reading this semester?" Julian asked.

"Honestly, Mr. D, I don't even have any idea of it yet. You would send us a list to our homes in the summer, but not Ms. Burks. She wants to 'get to know us' as people or something and call her 'Jan.' The worst thing is she doesn't use deodorant and she eats at her desk. Pumpkin seeds or something like an actual bird, and she sure does look like one, if you ask me and most of the other kids in the class who call her the Bird Lady. I'll be surprised if there is any reading involved because it might take a really long time getting to know each other. What does that even mean and what ever happened to Charles Dickens?"

Not knowing quite how to answer that question or determine if it was in fact rhetorical, Julian just shook his head in keeping with the spirit of Donna's indignation.

"Don't worry, kid. They are going down or I'll die trying and I don't plan on dyin'. So, just hold tight, ya hear me?"

"Yes, I do, Miss Lois, yes I do."

"Ya hear me, Jules?"

"I hear you, Lois, I might not..."

"Shhhht, shut it down, my friend, you hear me, that's all I need to know."

When young Tibbets arrived on the tail end of another day in pursuit of truth, justice and the American way, he found his girlfriend and her former teachers trying to get a pile of red, polyester dinner napkins to hold the fan shape. This table linen sleight of hand was Donna's mother's pride and one of the many such dubious skills she had tried to pass along to her daughter.

"Maybe we need to spray some Niagara on them," Donna said.

"What's Niagara?" Julian asked.

"Oh, Mr. D, don't you men ever learn household products or anything? You probably never even knew how to iron a tablecloth because if you did, maybe you used Niagara and found out it was starch to make things stiffer and hold up against getting all wrinkled up right away again."

"The kids got a point, Jules, and she said Niagara not Viagra, just so we're clear," Lois said as she apprised her friend with a mix of wise assery and mischievousness.

"How goes it, friends of my friend, teachers of the taught, masters of all things bar and grill and fellows of the table and the cloth?" said Tibbets, who then drew his porkpie hat from his head with a flourish and bowed deeply before them.

This delighted and impressed his girlfriend Donna who jumped up and rewarded her young swain with a bosomy hug. For a moment, Tibbets, who was a toothpick of a fellow, was nothing but head, neck and shoulders as he towered, and Donna enveloped.

Julian experienced a fleeting internal sigh. Love and romance seemed so far removed from his recent life and reminders of it like this made him wistful.

Lois just got up and joined the hug. She had grown quite fond of this young man and Donna for all her inscrutability had become something of a second, differently challenged daughter.

As any good reporter, Tibbets had come to his friends with something to report and was anxious to do so. His editor, he told them, had called him in to discuss his work on what the tow was lately referring to as the trial of the century, that being the impending fruit of Lois and Julian's lawsuit against the Fitzgerald's.

"He told me go ahead and write your puff pieces about Barcus B and G, but let's keep clear of the legal stuff involving two of its proprietors. I was shocked. So, I said to him, 'You mean I can't report the truth, Sir?' He said, 'Not when one of our best and only advertisers are upset that you seem to be favoring the other side.' 'Well, I resent that, Sir, with all due respect,' I told him, and he said, 'I know, I know, Tibbets, journalistic integrity and all that. But, look kid, what good is journalistic integrity if you don't have a journal? I have to be honest the Fitzgerald's have the power to make us or break us. So, we've got to back off; we have no choice.'"

As Lois and Julian shook their heads in disbelief, Donna grabbed a rare successful napkin fan and crumpled it in her fist, which she then banged against the table.

"The injusticeness!" she declared. "You're only trying to do the job that was expected of you to do and tell the true story of this, and what do you get? But no you can't do it because the Fitzgerald's have decided that no you cannot. I am so mad that I could bite my nails and spit them out."

"This doesn't surprise me one bit," Julian began and went on to lay out his argument for why he and Lois should give up this tilting at windmills, settle with the big, bad, powerful Fitzgerald's and move on with their lives.

"Not over my dead body!" Lois declared and this did not surprise Julian either.

Not one to await an invitation, Doreen sat down at the booth and joined the conversation. As she spoke, she whipped a couple dozen napkins into perfect fans without bothering to even look down at her handiwork. Her napkin folding talent was either practiced or innate, but either way, all present were left somewhat speechless by it. Doreen loved to talk, so others being speechless worked fine for her.

"So, you know who I happened to run into at the Fireman's Pancake Fundraising breakfast? Fitzgerald, your old boss, who fired you, that's who, and wanna know who else was there? Yours all lawyer, Snodgrass. And, yeah, you might be thinking big deal, so two people show up at the same place where there's a lot of people. But, what's weird is, I notice Fitzgerald goes to leave and then Snodgrass leaves right after him and I'm looking out the window to the parking lot area where everyone had to park so as not to block in any of the firetrucks and I see with my own eyes Snodgrass gets into the passenger seat of Fitzgerald's big ass luxury car. They sit talking for five, maybe ten, minutes and then Snodgrass gets out and comes back to have another plate of pancakes. I can't say as I blame him, they were good, really good. You could choose plain, banana, blueberry...."

"Hold on a minute, Doreen. First, we're really not interested in what kind of pancakes they were serving at the Fireman's Pancake Fundraiser, and second, what the hell were you doing there?"

"What I was doing is God's work, Lois. Ever heard of it? It's called a charity where going there and buying the pancakes is doing good for the needy who probably can't afford to eat pancakes and could use a little leg up."

"I think the world has had enough of your little legs up, Doreen."

"Very funny, Lois. At least I have legs to put up."

"You saying I don't have legs? Is that what you're trying to say?"

"Oh no, Lois. Nobody would ever accuse you of not having legs. Whether they can be lifted up or not is another question or whether anyone would want them to be, unlike my legs, I might add."

"What I'm going to add, Doreen, is I can lift you and your legs up no problem and toss you on out of here and back onto the trash heap you crawled out of."

"Ladies, please, enough. Doreen here may have some important information with regard to our lawsuit and I for one would rather listen to that than to you two going on about legs and pancakes. So, you saw Snodgrass having a chat with Fitz and then come back to the breakfast? Then what? You talk with him at all?"

"You can bet your cute, little bootie I talked to him, Julian. I just cozied up to him at the pancake bar and tried to be flirty, but not too flirty, just enough to get him off balance or like what I do with guys here, so they'll give me a bigger tip. I know what he was thinking too, he was thinking, 'Hey look at me. Maybe the rug I'm wearing to hide my baldness is not so bad. Maybe it's my casual look, my Saturday pants and a turtleneck might be sexier than the usual suit and tie.' Well, I'm pretty sure it was really a Dickies, which I prefer anyways. I know he was thinking this because I could tell he was real pleased with himself."

"Okay, so Snodgrass was flattered. What happened then, Doreen? This is important, you understand?"

"Yes, I do understand, Mr. Big Shot English Teacher, why you think I went to all that trouble. Flirting with Snodgrass, are you kidding me? You gotta be kidding me."

"Sorry, sorry, I'm just really interested in what you're telling us, Doreen."

"Well, then let me talk and try not to insult me then, okay?"

"Sorry, okay."

"I'm like 'Have you tried the blueberry.' He's like 'I'm more of a banana man myself.' And gives me a wink like this is supposed to mean something more than just a selection of pancake toppings. I act like it's funny what he said and give one of my cute little laughs and he invites me to sit with him and, more importantly, does go ahead and gets a blueberry pancake."

Julian was keeping a close eye on Lois who looked to be inching back to her tipping point. Donna started in on her manicured nails. Tibbets, who was writing all this down in his spiral bound five by si reporter's notepad, held pen over paper as if frozen in time.

Doreen, knowing that she had her audience in the palm of her hand, milked this pause, pulled a Virginia Slim out of her purse, lit it with her pink Bic and asked Julian to fetch her an ashtray. This he did at warp speed. Doreen inhaled with concentrated intent and blew out smoke rings that were far less impressive than her napkins.

"So, you could say I've got him where I want him, if you know what I mean?"

Doreen looks around the table to ascertain the degree to which this impresses her audience.

"Yes, yes, we know, Doreen, we know what you mean."

"Well, thank you, Professor, a girl can appreciate being understood. So, anyway, like I said, he loves the pancakes and especially after I take the thing of syrup and pour more of it real slow for him over his plate and then let some of it pour down on my finger and lick it, kind of sexy like this. Hello, you see how I did that? Sexy right?"

"Yes, really sexy, Doreen, the sexiest."

"I like a man of good taste and appreciation, Julian. I really do. So, anyways, as I was saying, Snodgrass is like putty in my hand at this point in time and I go ahead and ask him how the lawsuit is going and how fascinating I think it is that's he's a lawyer and everything and that I never met a real lawyer before, which was a lie, but I wasn't about to tell him that. 'Well, don't you look nice, Mr. Attorney, Sir?' I say. 'How's that lawsuit of yours coming along? I bet you're going to make those Fitzgerald's pay big time. I guess my friends are about to be rolling in it. But I can't really even call them my friends if you know what I mean.' And he says, 'Hey, hello to you too. I thought you were all like one big happy family. Lois, Julian, Mitch and you.' 'Not guilty, your honor,' I said, kind of playing up the whole legal side of things. 'They are so not my friends. All I see is a couple of users, living off of the niceness of my ex husband. I see a big ol' lesbo and a little teensy puppy dog of a man, if you can call it that, doing whatever Lois tells him.' 'Well then, I guess the state drops all charges against you'" he tells me. 'And here I thought you and Julian might have something going on between you.' 'Oh pullease,' I tell him. "Julian? You ever see somebody so short? He's like a midget or something without actually being one. I like my men tall and strong, and for them not to be besties with giant, pushy, diesel dykes."

"Sorry, Julie, I had to make him think I was not on your guyses side."

"And what about me?" Lois asked between tightly clenched teeth.

"What about you, Lois?"

"You're something, Doreen, you know that. But forget about it, I'll extract my apology another day. Let's just get on with it please."

"Well aren't you all polite saying please to little old me. I think that might be the first polite thing you've ever said to me, Lois."

"Good, okay, now what did he say? Snodgrass, what did he say to you?"

"Well, first, I said to him that he had nothing to worry about telling me what's happening with the case because I really couldn't care less about you two, but I always had an interest in legal matters and especially in the lawyers who conducted them."

Doreen paused to see if her atypically articulate communication was being fully appreciated.

"He said these are complicated matters and that he could tell I was a really smart girl, but that he wouldn't think of trying to bore me with all the boring details. 'You can't bore me, Mr. Lawyerman,' I tell him. 'I bet you could read me the phonebook and even if it was just the phonebook it wouldn't be boring.' I said. And boy did he eat that up. So, it's going along real good, and then Mitch decides to come over with another piping hot stack and puts it down on the table and invites himself to sit with us without asking, just at the wrong time. I tell him to go get us a refill of the syrup and Snodgrass takes this little minute alone again to hand me his engraved business card printed on the finest stock of paper and ask me to come by his office on Saturday and he'll walk me through the latest details of the lawsuit and buy me some lunch. And I say, 'You're open on Saturday,' and he says, 'For you I am,' and then Mitch comes back and that's that... Any more napkins to fold?"

Julian made it his business to be Doreen's handler in the plot to expose Snodgrass if, in fact, he was double-crossing them. It was Julian who would drop off Doreen for her Saturday rendezvous and would admonish her to not sacrifice too much for the cause.

The idea of the wire came from Tirana whose ex-husband, the cop, was able to provide the hardware. Though Lois thought it best that she be the one to back up Doreen, the designated plant put the kibosh on that notion.

"I'm not placing my safety and my honor in the hands of some ham hock who don't care if I'm dead or alive."

"First of all, bitch, I don't know who you're calling a ham hock or what that's even supposed to mean, but besides that, your honor? You did say your honor, didn't you?"

"Yes, my honor, Lois. Something you would know very little about."

"You sure got that right, Doreen. I wouldn't know a thing about your honor since as far as I can tell you don't have any."

"Hey, what happened to 'we're all just one big family?'" Mitch asked.

"Don't worry, Mitch," Julian pitched in. "I got this. I'm accompanying Doreen and I'll be parked right outside Snodgrass's door. He tries any funny business, he'll have me to answer to."

"Oohhh that's some scary fighting words coming from a beast like yourself, Julie."

"Enough, Lois, enough with the put downs and little man jokes. We have to handle this situation delicately. If we're wrong about Snodgrass and he finds out we're screwing around, we're you-know-whatted."

"Fucked, Jules? Is that what you're trying to say?"

"Watch your language, Lois. There's a lady present."

"Oh, so now Doreen is a lady, is it? Doreen's a lady and you're Superman and I guess I'll be Lois friggin Lane?"

"You can be whatever you want to be," Doreen piped in. "But Lois Lane was no lesbian."

"Oh yeah, and how do you know?"

"Everybody knows, Lois. All you need is half a brain in your head."

"At least I have a brain in my head, Doreen."

Barcus barked, causing the group to notice smoke billowing from the oven.

"You trying to cook again, Doreen."

"My muffins. Now you gone and made me burn my muffins, Lois."

The bottom quarter of the muffins having survived the flames, Julian bravely consumed one and hastened to compliment the chef.

"Blueberry-corn? My favorite."

"Actually, they're cinnamon apple, but I'm glad you like them, Professor."

"Crunchy, I like the crunch."

One, "Huh," muttered mid-week as Doreen was again remarking on her own cleverness was about as close as Lois got to confessing a tinge of admiration. The "huh" did not go unnoticed and had moved Doreen to retreat a word or two from her war of them with her archrival.

Julian and Mitch took this as a flicker of harmony to come, but weren't so foolish as to flat out say so. The fragile balance between Doreen and Lois was almost upset by Lois's daughter Shelley who was unquestionably taken with the newly deputized defender of the cause. Both sensing that this would drive Lois nuts and finding that Shelley made for a compliant disciple, Doreen was all in.

"What the hell have you done to your face?" Lois asked when her daughter walked out of Mitch's quarters with enough pancake make-up on to stucco a small wall.

Heavy black mascara extenuated Shelly's already long lashes, her lids were unnaturally blue and her lips a glistening and frosty hot pink.

"And why you walking so funny? What's those things on your feet?"

"Doreen and me had a beauty session is all, Mama. I like it, so don't even."

"Doreen? Doreen and you had a beauty session? Hah."

"Mama, shut it now. Don't go being all mean just because you don't happen to be a make-up wearer. I like it. Nobody showed me how to do it before and I like doing it so just let me, okay?"

Doreen took this opportunity to slide into the booth next to her protégé' to better come to her defense.

"Look, Lois" she said. "We all know that lesbians don't wear makeup or high heels or anything very, you know, girly like. But Shelley here, and I'm sorry to be the one to break it to you in case you didn't already know, your daughter, she's not a lesbian. She's a real girl, see?"

"I'll 'real girl' you, Doreen. You think lesbians don't wear makeup and aren't real girls? Well, I guess you think Tirana's not a real girl? You think Tirana's not way more of a real girl than you'll ever be and wears makeup like, let's see, Portia De Rossi and other famous people throughout history? You think you have a corner on the market? You think you straights are the only ones know how to wear high heels just because I prefer to not break the hundreds of little tiny bones we have in our feet trying to impress some loser of a man? No, thank you very much, Doreen. Thanks, but no thanks."

"Well then, you're not welcome then, Lois."

"Mama, please, it's okay. I accept you just like you are and I love you very much and I do not care one bit about if you wear lipstick or sneakers or anything you want. I just have to be me, like you've always said. 'You just be true to you, kid.' How many times have you said that to me, Mama? 'Just be true to you, kid.'"

"She looks nice, Lo," Julian interjected, chancing he'd incur Lois's wrath, but speaking from the heart nonetheless. "Donna wears makeup, right? Most girls their age wear it and Shelley is what? Four, five years older?"

Shelley mouthed a thank you to Julian that luckily passed her mother's attention.

"I'll thank you to stay right out of this, Julian. Shelley might be twenty two, but she's still just a senior in High school on account of her challenges. And besides, this is a conversation between mother and daughter, not mother and daughter and some wise guy who might be a good English Literature teacher, but knows nothing, nothing about women."

"Well, he sure knows how to treat a woman better than some women I know," Doreen chimed in.

"Mama, don't respond to that. Take a deep breath please. Look, I'm your kid and I love you and, to me, you're the best mom on earth, but Mama, makeup comes off, being the best mother does not."

Rather than breathe deep, Lois opted to down the shot Mitch had wisely slid in front of her. The warm glow of the Tequila made up the small gap between Shelley's sweet pronouncement and Lois's umbrage. The trick was done and so had ended yet another cat conflagration at Barcus Bar and Grill.

Apart from the big event to come, the sting operation itself, this small victory capped off a week of heady self-importance. And eventually, even Lois had to admit that what Doreen had stumbled on and set in motion at the Fireman's Pancake Breakfast was uncharacteristically helpful. She had to keep it to herself, but she was moved to admit that Doreen was showing some unexpected guile.

CHAPTER Nine

The following Saturday, Tirana's ex, Teddy, showed up with the official government-issued wire to prepare Doreen for her first, and perhaps last, undercover mission.

"It's so very nice to be on the right side of the law for a change," Doreen flirted.

Teddy was just the sort of big, strapping, soft spoken guy that most warm-blooded females responded to with little reserve. He had a Barry White kind of baritone and mystique without the Barry White waistline. Doreen was quite thrilled by the close physical contact necessary to the proper installation of the device. Teddy apologized for the intrusion and was quickly assured by Doreen that he was just doing his job.

"Believe me, I've had worse," Doreen joked with a wink and one of her inexplicable baby doll pouts.

"Doreen, try to stay still now," Teddy warned as he fished shallowly in the vicinity of Doreen's cleavage.

"Yessir, Mr. Officer. Anything you say, Sir."

"You don't have to call me Officer."

"Roger that, Captain. (tee-hee). Aren't I just a handful?"

"Yes, yes you are, Doreen."

"Umm, no disrespect, Ted, aren't there more modern forms of stealth recording devices? I think my ex-wife used one on me, but it wasn't attached to her body or anything," Julian said as he insinuated himself between Teddy and Doreen.

"Look, you can go spend money on a pen device or a button device. There's all kinds of devices these days, but this here is the real Magilla. This is what we used when I was on the force and it still works good today."

"Didn't you retire like twenty-five years ago?"

"Hey, you want to go to the detective store and get some over the counter gizmo, with about zero reliability, for hundreds of bucks? Suit yourself."

"No, no, it's fine. You're the expert. How's it feel, Kid?"

"Well, it feels just fine, Professor. Don't you go worrying about me."

"I'm not worried, really I'm not. Anything goes wrong, Barcus and I have your back."

"I still say, I shoulda been the one doing the backup. Something happens, it just might take a little more strength and size than what I'm looking at right here. Just sayin," Lois interrupted.

"Well, you can just forget about that, my homosexual friend, not. You think I'd leave my safe being up to you? You gotta be high on glue."

"High on glue, is it? What's that feel like, Doreen? Cause you're the one who would know anything about high on glue, not me. You high on glue right now? How's that feel? You need a little Elmer's before you go on your dangerous mission with the big, bad, hairless lawyer, who has about as much muscles as a bowl of ramen noodles?"

"Hey, Lois, the only thing I'm sniffing is not noodles and it's not glue. What I'm sniffing is sniffing out a rat. I'd like to see you do that, Lois. I'd like to see you sniff out a rat by being all cute and flirty-like. Then, I really would be high on glue if I ever saw that."

Only Julian noticed Teddy slipping out the front door. He gave his pal a thumbs up in a way of wishing him luck. Julian nodded and thumbed back.

"Ok, you two, if there was ever a time to declare a truce, it's now. I tell you what, Lois, you stay here and mind the shop, but make sure to be close by the phone in case I need backup. And don't worry about me. If I have to use some of my old wrestling moves, I know I can do that."

"You haven't wrestled since Jr. High, Julian. And if you were so great, why'd you quit after Jr. High? Lemme guess, you were too short, even for wrestling."

"That's it. I've had more than enough of your disrespect, my friend. You don't know anything about my wrestling career, alright? So just mind your own business. And another thing, you say anything else about my height and I'll come right back at you about your width. So, cool it."

"Well, I, for one, just think I'm in perfectly good hands, aren't I?"

"Shut up, Doreen," Lois and Jules pronounced in unison.

As usual, Mitch stayed out of the fray. It was a little early to be serving up alcohol, which was normally his contribution to quiet Lois down.

"Chamomile tea, anyone?"

"Shut up, Mitch," replied the three.

Snodgrass's office was just around the corner from the main street in town. The taxi driver, who was hardly satisfied with the extra five buck tip that had bought passage for Julian's giant dog, dropped them by the small park that was the village square. A statue of Samuel H. Fitzgerald I astride a bucking steed loomed ominously in the center. Julian picked a bench where he couldn't be gazed upon by his adversary's legendary relation. They were a half hour early, but Julian liked to be prepared.

"Ok, he said to Doreen. "We need to have a safe word in case anything goes wrong."

"A safe word? What's a safe word, Professor? You're the word person around here."

"It's a special word you say if you're in trouble. It can be any word, just so long as we both know what that word is and Snodgrass doesn't."

As they spoke, a local pigeon delivered a small splat on Julian's shoe.

"Ok, how about 'Bird poop?'"

"'Too long.'"

"'Shoe pant.'"

"Kind of difficult to remember."

"Well then, how about 'dimple' 'cause I'm looking at a very cute one in the middle of your chin and I have two on my face that are cute also."

"I like it. Dimple. 'Dimple' it is. You say the word 'dimple' and we'll come running, but hopefully you won't have to say it."

"But, I like to say it. Dimple; it's cute."

"Yes, but it's just for saying if there's trouble, okay?"

"Oh, okay, be like that, Mr. party-pooper."

"After this, you can say "dimple' all you want. It's just for today."

"If you say so, with that cute hmmm on your chinny chin chin. Tee hee."

Julian was fully aware that this was serious business, but Doreen's light heartedness brought a smile to his lips. He hoped to God that all would go without a hitch as he sent his brave agent on her way. After clocking three minutes exactly in strict adherence to the reconnaissance conducted by dark of night a few days before, Julian popped in his ear plugs and began tuning his police issue relic of a thirty-year-old transmission device.

He felt confident and exhilarated somehow.

"This would be better than a Bond film," he thought.

It would be like being in a Bond film, as if he were Bond himself. The best part, which he could only dare to consider, was that his undercover colleague was growing in his affection; more and more each day. But that presented a whole other kind of danger, which needed to be set aside in deference to the mission at hand.

Julian watched hungrily as the diminutive Doreen and her bouncy little ass hobbled away down the street and out of sight. Julian found her courage to be irresistible and could vouch for her recent statement that 'she'd never met a man she couldn't tame.'

Doreen approached the venerable old brick building, a former bank that had been converted into offices. She hesitated just for a breath at the base of the wide marble steps.

"Here's goes nothin'," she whispered as she made a perfunctory and completely botched sign of the cross.

She couldn't help observing that the mix of trepidation and exhilaration were as good as any first hit of glue. She pressed the buzzer for Snodgrass and soon heard steps bounding down a creaky wooden stairway. Snodgrass threw open the door and wrapped his long arms around Doreen with plenty of arm to spare. Defensively and in fear that he may immediately detect the hardware under her top, Doreen created a barrier with her fists.

"Well, hello to you too, Mr. Legal Eagle. Now, careful now. I'm just a little bit and you almost knocked me off your front porch here. Tee-hee."

"I'm just that happy to see you, Doreen. It's rare to find a woman who takes an interest in my complex line of work, and who knows more than a thing or two about how to eat a pancake, I might add. Now, come on with me, little lady, and let me introduce you to my humble abode; the place where the magic happens."

"How'd you know I'm a big magic lover? You must be a sidekick or something," Doreen gushed.

"Hah, that's a good one. A psychic in search of a sidekick you might say. Anyway, let me show you around."

"Reception area, where some people have to wait for quite a while, and some, such as yourself, not one little bit."

Doreen looked around and was impressed with the green leather, walnut trimmed couch, with all the brass grommets.

"Pure Perry Mason," she thought.

The glass coffee table held a variety of reading materials like The Massachusetts Law Review, National Geographic and even Readers Digests, serendipitously Doreen's favorite source of literature not counting True Detective, which Snodgrass did not have. There was a lovely old black and white photo depicting the square and the very building in which she stood from back in the early 1800's. She noted the metal and fiberboard reception desk, which didn't quite meet up to the overall gravitas, but featured a modest curtain, which was a nice touch. A supply of Werther's originals sat on the desk in a cut glass candy dish. Thoughtful. The floor was highly polished brown linoleum tile on which one might be able to hear high heels coming from about a mile away. Snodgrass turned the brass knob to a half snowflake motif, opaque glass and half oak door. Doreen got a whiff of old, which she preferred to interpret as historical rather than musty.

Underfoot, she found herself treading on wide planks of glossy pine with a virtual minefield of plug holes and irregularities. She began to see why office women brought sneakers to work, but was vaguel unsettled by this thought when she remembered that usually it was the other way around; sneakers on the way to work, heels at work.

"Whatever," she dismissed the contradiction by figuring it all depended on what kind of office and it could go either way.

Meantime, she warned herself to stop thinking and pay attention or she might not make it to the swivel armchair with brass hooded wheels to which Snodgrass directed her. It was settled in front of a large oak desk with a big piece of glass on it and green felt in between. Doreen plopped herself down less gingerly than was wise.

Understandably, she was eager to not have to balance on the narrow stems of her ill-advised footwear. What she didn't count on was that the chair back rested on a spring-loaded neck that responded to weight by tilting backwards, way backwards. So far backwards, in fact, that Doreen and chair went quite violently topsy turvy so that she remained seated, but with her legs in the air and by grace of the support of her neck and shoulders smooshed against the floor. Add to this that she was blinded by her skirt over her head and add to that the fact that this sight so distracted Snodgrass that he was very, very slow to come to the rescue. Once he'd gotten her and the chair upright, Snodgrass chivalrously bent to screw in a knob that apparently reduced the spring action. They both apologized more or less at once and then Doreen broke into one of her uncontrollable laughing fits, which lasted beyond what might be considered normal.

Snodgrass joined in the mirth momentarily before becoming alarmed enough by Doreen's hysteria to find himself slipping into his 'Thank God I have insurance. She might be concussed' arena.

He proffered a handkerchief with which Doreen daubed her eyes in between fresh outbursts. She almost fell out of the chair a second time with no need of help from the furniture itself. Snodgrass passed her a glass of water and, after a sip or two, she was able to collect herself sufficiently to ask if he had something stronger. He obliged with a generous splash of Jack Daniels, one for her and one for himself, and order was temporarily restored.

Doreen's tumble had transmitted as an earsplitting crash to Julian in the park. The hairs on his arms stood at attention as, in response, did Barcus's ears. Julian wondered if this was it, his call to action, or whether patience and trust should hold him in place until more was revealed. He heard the sound of swallowing, clear as a bell and a somewhat reassuring purr of what he distinguished as contentment. But not too much contentment he hoped. And then, it came to him: little crazy as a fruitcake, superstitious, whack-a-mole Doreen had captured his heart. Her approval, attention, well-being and acceptance had become his most important thing.

How this was possible, he couldn't begin to understand. She was conveniently petite, yes, but that alone couldn't possibly cover it. He tried to imagine a conversation with her; any conversation, which he'd found enlightening, inspiring, compelling. He got nothing. And yet, she moved him somehow. He wanted to protect her from the harsher realities she chose to ignore or was simply unaware of. He wanted her not to lose the certainty with which she was convinced of her own seat at the table. He needed somehow to prove to her that he too deserved his and was therefore worthy of her affection.

A car whooshed by sending up a spray from a roadside puddle that almost hit him and his trusty dog. Momentarily, this seemed to bring him to his senses.

"What a load of nonsense," he thought.

As if Doreen was anywhere near an appropriate match for an intellectual such as himself.

"Ludicrous! I must be feeling desperate!"

The pounding of his heart was everything to do with the mission at hand and certainly not with anything as nuts as he, Julian, falling for her, Doreen.

Her sweet, if nasally, voice came to him. For better or for worse, order seemed to have been restored at the epicenter of the mission. That said, the familiar twang was uncharacteristically muffled. He played with the antenna to the recording device and watched the tape loop like a sluggish knitting wheel. He removed the bulky headphones for a second to tap at them in hopes of deriving clearer audio, but the under-waterish quality did not improve. "Equipment fuck up! Great!"

It would require all of his concentration to pick up just the general tone of what was being said.

"No time for romantic excursions of the mind, Romeo."

It was near impossible for Julian to perceive that Doreen had deftly turned the conversation to the all-important topic of the lawsuit.

"I just want to pick that gigantic brain of yours," she had teased. "And, just so you know, I really don't think that that lot of fools is any match for Fitz who just happens to be the richest man in town, even if they have a great lawyer such as yourself, no offense."

"None taken, none taken. My big brain, as you call it, comes with a matching ego."

"Oh and you're a wise ass too, I see, Mr. Bigshot. Tee-hee."

"I'll be that too, if that's what you want. Geez, you're adorable. Do you have any idea how adorable you are?"

"Well, flattering will get you anywhere, Mr. Snodgrass, but I'm here to learn what my future holds and I don't think it holds Mitch or millions of dollars coming our way because of this lawsuit. I might not look like the most educated girl on the planet, but my GED means something and it tells me that you are too smart to be on the wrong team. So, I'm here for you to give me the inside scoop. And, by the way, I know you had a meeting with Fitz at the Pancake Breakfast 'cause I saw it with my own little old eyes."

"Hah, so you're as clever as you are cute, is that it? But I bet you one thing, Little Lady, you think I'm smart, you have no idea, no idea at all. You think I sold out to Fitz, don't you? You think I took a bribe from the junior representative of the only family in town that has refused to ever use my good services? You think I jumped at the chance to kiss their ass and be in their pockets? C'mon confess. That's what you think, isn't it?"

"Yeah, well, maybe, but I'm here to tell you I don't blame you even one little bit. Dogs eat dogs don't they? My Mama used to tell me 'Doree' (she called me Doree) 'Doree,' she says. 'There are two kinds of people in this world, the ones that do good so they'll make it to heaven when they die and the one's are too smart to wait. You see a chance to get ahead in life, you grab it with both hands. I don't care where that opportunity comes from. You grab it, hear me?' she'd say. 'No sense worrying about heaven when not a single person you'll ever meet can actually say they've been there and that it even exists.'"

"Wise Mom. So, you're gonna like this. I happen to have known what Fitz wanted to speak with me in private about. That didn't take much brain power, you see, but what Fitz didn't know is that I taped our conversation."

"You wore a wire?"

"A wire? Who wears a wire? I recorded it on my Apple Watch."

Doreen fumbled in her purse and retrieved a lipstick stamped kleenex tissue with which she dabbed at the droplets of sweat that had begun to form on her very red face. Snodgrass grabbed the glass of water that sat on his desk and rushed around to offer it.

"You okay there? Here, let's take off this heavy jacket."

"No, no, I'd get a chill without it. Trust you me, I'm just fine. I just need you to direct me to the little girl's room please."

"Oh, okay, I get it. My wife used to get this when she was going through the change."

"Going through the change, at my age? You gotta be kidding me. You may be smart about some things, but, geez, you think a woman in her late twenties, such as me, would be going through the change?"

"Ahhh, sorry, sorry, no offense. What do I know? Here, this way, just down the hall and to the left."

Doreen chose the first of two stalls. She wished for a moment that she had a good old bag of glue. As undignified a drug as that seemed, it was still her favorite. She couldn't help herself. Thankfully, she'd hopped a ride on the vanity wagon long ago because, truth be told, she'd been in her late twenties for quite a few years now.

Maybe it was a hot flash. She had to consider that possibility and that the sticky wire receptors that had slid down beneath her boobs and were only being held in place by her bra and the bulky recorder thing around her waist made her extra pissed off.

Jacket off, she began to cool down a little, but she tore at the apparatus with a vengeance and tossed it into her bag. She threw the jacket over که, washed her face, sneered briefly at the Tampon machine on the wall and made her way back to Snodgrass.

Julian was baffled and alarmed at all the unintelligible sounds feeding into his ears. Was that a toilet flush? Again, he was confronted with indecision. Spring into action or wait it out? But there were the voices again, so muffled that he could no longer make out a single word and yet the tone and cadence assured him that nothing violent was likely taking place. He let the headphones rest on his shoulders and shared a salami sandwich with Barcus.

Doreen was not kidding when she told Snodgrass she wouldn't blame him if he took a bribe from Fitz. She figured that anything that was picked up on the recording could be denied as a ploy to get Snodgrass to talk. She was certain Julian would give her the benefit of the doubt. It was obvious to her that she had the little guy wrapped around her finger. And she liked him alright, but figured Snodgrass might be more her speed. She and Mitch were done, she knew that much.

Over a room temperature bottle of Zinfandel (her favorite) and some packets of Keeblers Cheese and Peanut Butter Crackers (also her favorite), Snodgrass made it clear just how good her options really were.

His intention was to go with his damning recording, not to Fitz, but to Fitz's father, a hard ass New England patriarch who had made it his life's work to redeem the blue blood status and reputation of his family and to expunge the taint left by his grandfather's rum running and other nefarious means of acquiring jaw dropping amounts of wealth. He calculated that such a man would not endorse bribery of any kind and that, if by chance he had, anyone finding out about it would probably be the death of him. Snodgrass would suggest that all would be forgotten and the tape would not be introduced at trial if, in fact, there were no trial and assuming as he did that his clients would be quite open to a generous settlement.

Doreen almost fell out of her seat for a second time all over again. Meanwhile, Julian remained in his: the bench in the park. He consulted his watch frequently and was tiring of the dull hum that he had hoped would be thrilling dialogue. So much for undercover work. Now he knew that those who had warned that it was nothing like what you see on TV were absolutely right. He would have been excited to know what Doreen had just found out and would have been thrilled to have heard them go on.

"Well, I'll be, Mr. Snodgrass, I think you are Alfred E. Einstein or somebody. Holy geez, I'm trying to wrap my head around it and, for the first time in my life, I think, I don't know what to say. Why? Let me ask you that. Why go to all this trouble to win for those, well, let's be honest here, losers such as Lois and not just take the bribe and cash in?"

"Can I say because I'm a good guy? Maybe, but I'm not that good. A couple of things; I'm working for those losers as you refer to them on contingency, whatever they get combined, I get half of all of it to myself. Fitz Jr. has access to funds, but he'd never be able to scrape together enough to match the amount his daddy could pony up and that's assuming, you understand, that his dear old dad doesn't have a clue about this. And last, but not least, I'd like to take it to the man who thought that I was just some local schmuck and has always overlooked me to go give all of his business, and I mean all of it, to those high-priced stuffed shirts in Boston. After this, I'm not going to need his business; I'm not even going to want any of it. It's Vegas for me, baby. I'm buying off my wife and heading west; sunshine and casinos, no more shoveling snow and shuffling papers."

"Vegas?"

"Yeah, Vegas."

"Oh."

The very mention of Vegas left Doreen feeling a little wobbly, a bit off her game. It's true she thought hopefully that what happens there stays there, but that could only mean that it would all be waiting for her if she ever dared go back. For one, she might run into her ex. That was deterrent enough, but add her various financial obligations to gentlemen of a questionable character and the admonishment of the kind officer who had escorted her to the bus depot and sent her on her way with a warning never to return and Vegas was definitely off Doreen Kaliboski O'Gorman's list of desirable locales.

"Vegas, huh, you're sure about that?"

"Yeah, I thought you loved Vegas."

"It was great for my career and everything, being a showgirl and a so-called headliner, if you have to know, and I don't mean to brag. But life in the limelight takes its toll on a girl. I found myself missing the simple country enjoyments like flowers on a bush instead of giant bouquets waiting in my dressing room every night."

"I bet you could have opened a flower shop."

"I'm thinking Florida, maybe the Tampa Bay area. I hear it's nice."

"No way. It's Vegas or bust for me, Little Lady. I've dreamt about living in the desert since I was just a little kid. I had an Uncle Milty used to come from there. The guy knew how to live. Never worked a day in his life and had more money than all three of his brothers put together. Anyway, that's my plan."

"Well, good for you then. I hope you like it. Meanwhile, I best be on my way and I thank you, kind gentleman, for your cordiality."

"What? You're leaving already?"

"Got to go make the donuts. You'd think they could run that place without me, but you would be sadly mistaken, Mister."

"You could call in sick. I wanted to take you to a nice place in Stockbridge for dinner."

"Well, isn't that a thought, going out for a change and getting waited on for once. But, you know me, Miss Responsibility. One of my Mama's boyfriends actually named me that under circumstances that were so silly I'm not even going to get into them. But the name stuck, I guess."

"I won't insult you by trying to insist, but I have two demands."

"I'm listening."

"You let me drive you home and you promise to let me take you out on a real date one of these days."

"Today might just be your lucky day Mr. Snodgrass 'cause you got yourself two whole yesses."

Julian did not have eyes on the building so he failed to see Doreen emerge on Snodgrass's arm and disappear around the corner.

The sound in the earphones faded to something shy of white noise. This concerned him gravely. It was one thing to pick up the sing-song of a cordial adult conversation, even if the words were unintelligible, but it was quite another to suddenly register utter silence. Something wasn't right. In all likelihood, the wire had been discovered. How? He couldn't say, but in what other way could he explain the sudden silence. It was past time to sit around and wait for a signal. Obviously, Doreen was no longer in a position to send one. It was the moment he had both dreaded and desired. It was time for action. Julian gave Barcus a pat on the head and held a finger to his lips so the dog wouldn't bark. Nonetheless, Barcus barked, not once, but many times as his master had startled him out of a delightful nap.

Julian steeled himself and thought with gratitude about the fortifying sandwich he had consumed not long before. Who knew what he was about to get into the middle of? He would need his strength. Thinking quickly, he took off the headphones and shoved them and the recorder under the park bench. Taking hold of Barcus's leash as gingerly as possible so as not to get him too excited again, he began to take determined steps towards Snodgrass's building. When they reached the corner, he pressed his back against the exterior wall as he had seen cops do in movies. Barcus hadn't seen cops do this in movies and continued along mid sidewalk as per normal.

From a certain angle, it looked like a giant dog was walking himself on a leash suspended from thin air. Man and dog ascended the wide exterior stairs, the former as surreptitiously as possible, the latter not so much.

Then, our hero found himself face to face with those giant doors, doors not at all unlike the ones at Fitz Prep. Doors carved and fitted no doubt by the same sadistic and very tall craftsman.

"God dammit to hell," Julian hissed.

Pumping himself up to his ultimate stature, he stretched for the brass lever. He tugged with all his might, but couldn't get sufficient leverage to exert enough downward pressure, or so he thought because, truth told, the door was locked tight and even the tallest of Julians could not have opened it.

He buzzed every buzzer to no effect. He eyed a trash receptacle nearby. This might have worked as a platform, but such local amenities had been anchored to the sidewalks after a group of drunken pranksters, in fact former students of Julian's, had decided it would be fun to knock them all over and leave a bunch of garbage spilled out on the street at the peak of leaf changing season when the mess would have maximum impact on the scant, but much needed tourist trade. With tremendous regret, Julian pulled out his phone and dialed the restaurant.

"Barcus B+G, we don't take reservations."

"What do you mean we don't take reservations, Lois? We take reservations, you know that."

"Well, if it isn't James Bond 007 himself. For you, sir James, no reservation is required. Yeah, I know we take reservations, Julian, but we're booked solid and I figure any schmuck who thinks we don't take reservations will show up and we can seat them at the bar. Marketing 101. Where the hell are you?"

"Where am I? I'm outside of Snodgrass's building and I need backup. I think Doreen is in trouble."

"Really? Did you go inside and check?"

"I'm having a little difficulty accessing the premises."

"What another tall doorknob?"

"Don't start."

"I know, I know, just kidding, my friend. Well, look here, I've got some really good news for you, secret agent man. Doreen is right here standing next to me and she's just fine."

CHAPTER Ten

Julian and Barcus sat outside on those broad stone steps for a long time, partly because Julian was beyond dejected, but also because the Uber service in that neck of the woods was 'I could have walked there faster' slow. He normally would have recognized the royal blue Camry, but he was lost in disappointment. He opened the back door and stuck his head in to ask if Barcus would be welcome and was prepared for a knock down drag out if the answer was "no."

"Oh, hey Tibbets. Hey, Donna. C'mon, boy, hop in."

"Well, hey back to you, even though it's for horses, Mr. D. Whatever can you be doing in this place at this hour of the day when nothing is open here?"

"It's a long story."

"Is it by any chance fit for print, Mr. D?" Tibbets asked.

"No, kid, it is definitely not fit for print. Do me a favor and pull up over here while I retrieve something I left under that bench."

"Woooh, sure is sounding more and more like a mystery to me, Mr. D, almost like that Sherlock Holmes you made us read."

"Well, no, it's nothing like Sherlock Holmes, just some nonsense that I really don't want to get into, if you two don't mind. Okay?"

"Roger that, Jules. Where we headed?"

"Home."

"Home" was as busy as Julian had ever seen it. Tibbets had to park his Camry on a grassy incline at the far end of the gravel lot. The three along with Barcus scrambled up the hill and headed toward the bar and grill. Tibbets noted that the top half of the neon A of Barcus Bar and Grill was out so that the letter looked like a U.

"Better get that fixed, Mr. D or you'll find yourself getting a lot of Sharia Law types favoring the place."

"What in the heck are you saying now, Tibby? Me and Mr. D don't speak your silly talk, even if it can be cute sometimes."

"He's saying people are going to think it says Burkas, which by the way is fine with me. Come one, come all, I always say."

"Well, excuse you too, Mr. D, but how was I supposed to know that?"

"You weren't, kid, okay. Don't worry about it."

The place was so packed that no one could see Julian working his way through the crowd. When he reached the bar, Mitch threw him an apron and directed him to go over and man the service area. As Julian ascended to his platform and surveyed the crowd, he spotted Doreen talking up a bunch of beefy truck drivers, regulars, who she was keeping entertained while they put up with a long wait for a table. He tried to get her attention, but was quickly thwarted by Lois in full-on GO mode.

"Three lites, two pitchers, an Old Fashioned and a Rusty nail, Diet Pepsi, not Coke, no ice. And I ain't got all day."

"Wait, when the hell did Doreen get back here?"

"No time for trash talk. Get it? Trash talk? Anyways, my friend, we can save it for later. Right now, I got some thirsty customers that don't give two shits about Doreen and where and when that slut has or has not been."

Donna and Tibbets, far from sitting down for some free grub and a nice chat with their unusual adult friends, were put to work bussing tables, serving food and fetching checks. They were joined by Shelley, who had more or less finished with school and had opted to spend some time with her Mom. Clarissa Stuart was in the kitchen assembling towering club sandwiches with brightly colored cellophane frill topped toothpicks with which she repeatedly stabbed her fingers. The decks of turkey, bacon, lettuce, mayo and toast, which never did come together cooperatively enough to be presented to a paying customer, were cast aside. They would be consumed by the hungry and bedraggled staff, both permanent and temporary at the end of a blockbuster of a night.

The pace had been so insane that Julian temporarily forgot about the burning issue of what the hell had gone on with Snodgrass and Doreen, but only for a minute. He brought it up the instant they locked the front door behind the last customer.

Nobody wanted to hear about it. Count the money, have a sandwich and a drink or two and fall into bed was the simple consensus. They had made more money in one night than

Mitch had made for the entire year previous to this one—a new staircase worth of money at least. Business was good, life was good, and bed would be a great reward, except if you were Julian and spent the night making up conspiracy theories about Snodgrass and Doreen and feeling sorry for yourself.

Meanwhile, not very far up the road from Mitch's bustling joint was a venerable old prep school that had previously seen more vibrant days. Fitzgerald IV was loath to expel seven students who had been picked up by the police for drunk and disorderly behavior and soliciting drugs in the nearby city of Stockbridge. This one act of remediation would reduce the Sophomore class by an embarrassing amount. That's how far down enrollment had fallen in the wake of the Washington bus disaster. The school had become so desperate for paying students that they were content to accept those special kids who's disciplinary and or scholastic records had precluded them getting into any other school.

While his younger brother and nemesis was basking in the hugely successful opening of a luxury discount outlet at the edge of town, he would have to report this latest setback to his father, a task he considered with a violent shudder preceding a pity party that took him back over a long chain of childhood events in which he never succeeded in measuring up.

Everything had been going along reasonably well. In fact, better than expected until that fateful day. Much as his father would perceive that the buck stopped with him, all of Fitz IV's wrath fell squarely to Julian and Lois whose moronic ineptitude had ruined his life. Of course, he had no choice but to bribe Snodgrass. It would be worth every penny of his less than extravagant Trust to see those two held responsible, not just in the eyes of the law, but in those of the patriarch he so feared and from whom he so desperately sought approval.

Julian and Barcus were up at the crack of dawn, surprised to find Clarissa swooping around in the field behind the bar.

"Morning, Clarissa. You okay?"

"Okay, you ask, my friend, Okay? Just Okay? Well I'm wonderful, great, the best ever and more okay than this life has ever found me to be. I want to take you on a journey with me. Shall you come and put your hand in mine? May our four-legged Barcus be a beacon of benevolence. Yes you are, yes you are, big fellow, yes you are."

"Ahh, hmmm. Can I get you a cup of coffee, Clarissa?"

"Hah! Coffee! Who needs coffee?"

"But you love coffee. You always drink coffee, it's kind of your thing."

"My thing? My thing is not coffee, Sir. My thing is the universe and her majesty mother nature. Listen to the chirp, chirp, chirping of the birds, come place your hand on the earth and feel her beating heart. Come, don't be shy. She offers herself to you. Come."

After zero sleep and not in sufficient condition to argue, Julian bent down and placed his palm on the dirt. He did feel a thrumming, but was quite certain it corresponded to the size of the vehicle speeding along the nearby parkway at any given moment.

Whatever, if Clarissa wanted to think it was Mother Nature's beating heart, good for her. It was a great relief when he heard Lois' morning baritone.

"What the hell you doing, Jules, crouching around in the dirt?"

"Oh, hey, Lo; something's up with Clarissa."

"You can say that again. Where you been.? Something's been up with Clarissa for the last three weeks."

"Geez, I didn't know; guess I've been busy. What's the story?"

"I seen how busy you've been following that low life little piece of trailer trash Doreen around like a sick puppy. You can't fool me Julian; I know exactly how much of a fool you can be. My mistake to ever imagine that all men don't think alike."

"I don't know what you're talking about, Lois."

Clarissa, who had wandered off, came swooping back with a bedraggled bouquet of dandelions, which she proffered to Lois.

"Golden flowers for the Queen Mother of Barcus, blessed Bar and Grill."

"Oh, nice. Thanks, Princess, but you remember I told you the Queen Mother is allergic to weeds. Let Julian hold them for me. How you doin? Trippin' out of your mind again?"

"Oh yes, Goddess, I am trip, trip, tripping away. Yes I am, oh yes."

"She's tripping?"

"She's tripping."

"On LSD?"

"On mushrooms."

Julian found Doreen perched in a booth by one of the bay windows, staring out into the parking lot. As he approached, she instinctively went to plump up her hair.

This was made difficult by the fact that her head was festooned with large pink hair rollers huddled beneath a silk kerchief with an unlikely pairing of dolphins and lemon wedges. Her face looked erased by the lack of makeup, but Julian always had a favorable response to this. He liked the plain and simple version of Doreen even better than the one preferred by cosmetic companies. He was drawn to it without really knowing why and without really being able to put a finger on exactly what 'it' was. Just different, he thought.

"Well?" he said as he slipped into the booth opposite her.

"Well, what?" she said, still gazing out the window.

"What the hell happened?"

"I knew you were gonna ask me that. Can a girl just finish her first cup of coffee after a long hard day and night and would you be a peach and get me a refill and a jelly donut?"

"Okay, Doreen, but I really am anxious to get some answers here. Last time we talked, we were embarking on a critical and dangerous fact-finding mission. The equipment malfunctions somehow, I'm sitting in the park like a pervert with my headphones on listening to nothing but murmurings and such, and next thing I know I'm risking my own safety because I think you're in some kind of trouble, and cut to here: you are back at the place as if nothing ever happened. You have got to tell me what happened."

"Pretty please with a cherry on the top, more coffee and my donut first?"

"Alright, alright. I'll be right back."

As Julian headed toward the kitchen, he ran into Mitch still in his PJs, hair disheveled and eyeglasses at a severe tilt.

"Morning, Mitch."

"Morning, Jule. I thought I heard Clarissa out back."

"She is out back and Lois says she's tripping on psilocybin and I'm inclined to believe her."

"Oh, geez, she's doing it again."

"Again? You mean this is a regular thing for her?"

"Jules, ever since I cut it off with Clarissa out of respect for my marriage, she's been in a depression, a clinical depression, according to her. So, this headshrinker guru she's been following says to her to try this psychedelic stuff. It's makin' a comeback and has shown all kinds of great results in the treatment of people going through these things like she's been going through. Turns out it works, but I think it maybe works a little too good and she keeps showing up right under my nose acting all crazy and like life is all really great and everything. I'm afraid she's gonna spill the beans to Doreen. I don't know what she might say when she's in this state."

"Holy shit, Mitch, and you still have her working here?"

"Well, she still shows up and does her job, Jule. What can I do? Kick her to the curb?"

"No, like Lois says, you should save that for Doreen who walked out on you and took your house along with her. You two are over, Mitch. You've been over for a long time."

"Listen to me, buddy. I'm no saint, that's for sure, but I do believe in God and the Church and they tell me I made a vow and I have to stick to it. I have to confess, though, in all honesty, I still got it bad for that crazy Clarissa. Every time I see her, it's the same old feeling. I hope I can find a way to have that for Doreen again."

"It's not the kind of thing you can force, Mitch. If you have it, you have it. If you don't, you don't.

"You might be right, but my wife has asked me for a second chance here and, for all her faults, I don't want to be responsible for breaking her little heart."

"I think you're missing the big picture, pal."

"Well, like my Pa always said, 'Wallet size is plenty big enough for me.'"

"I guess."

Mitch continued out the door to intervene with his ecstatic ex. Julian shook his head and went to fetch Doreen's breakfast.

'Yumm, raspberry, my favorite."

"It's always raspberry, Doreen. You know that."

"Well, look who's being an old poopy pot this morning. I'm just saying raspberry is my favorite and that does not mean I'm saying that it is or is not always raspberry, Professor Bigshot."

"Sorry, you're right, Doreen. Now, can we please, please talk about what happened?"

"Well, I've got good news and bad news. Which do you want to hear first?"

"I really don't care, just tell me everything."

"Okay, but you have to pick."

"Alright, the bad news."

While sipping on that first cup of coffee and before encountering Julian, Doreen had had time to consider her position.

Ever since she had introduced the whole pancake breakfast scenario, she'd been taken seriously for a change. Even Lois had been required to back off some and show a smidgen of respect. If she now revealed everything Snodgrass had told her, that little bit of sunshine would go behind the clouds, quite possibly never to be seen again. There was that and the fact that she had promised Snodgrass not to spill the beans for fear his master plan would be leaked or thwarted in some way.

Despite the fact that Snodgrass would stand to get the biggest windfall and she liked the way he treated her, she had to admit he wasn't really her type, and being that he was hellbent on Vegas pretty much put the last nail in the coffin. Her half of Mitch's take would be plenty if it came to that. Marriage did have its advantages.

"I'm gonna have to go back in. I can't say for sure whether Snodgrass is on our side or not. I got him talking alright, but, with that damn wire sliding down the front of me, it was hard to work my magic, if you know what I mean."

"You weren't there to be working any magic, Doreen. You were there to find out what the hell our lawyer was up to."

Julian watched as Doreen tore off a piece of her donut and slowly licked out the jelly filling.

"If I can't work my magic, then how do you think I'm going to get through to a man like that? My magic, I'll have you know, is my secret weapon and I say that as a married woman who has learned the lessons of her past and would never work all of her magic with another man until she was officially divorced in the eyes of God if that was ever to happen."

"So, you got nothing?"

"I didn't say I got nothing, I said I had to go back in."

"Okay, so what did you get?"

"What I got is that Snodgrass admits to meeting with Fitz. That it was Fitz's idea and that it might look like funny business, but it wasn't. That he has a plan and that everyone is going to come out good in the end."

"That's it?"

"That's it. Oh and the other bad news is you're gonna have to buy me one of those computer watches so I can record whatever Snodgrass tells me the next time in the new and modern way."

"An Apple Watch?"

"One of those."

"Those things cost hundreds of bucks."

"That's why it's good that business is so good."

"You won't be able to have me as a back-up, you know, if we use an Apple Watch."

"Don't you worry, Professor, a good man like you can always be my backup, if you take my meaning. There any more of those donuts left?"

Julian was disappointed, not only had his protection services been rendered irrelevant, he had a vague suspicion that Doreen wasn't being entirely straight. Worse than that, and more to Julian's surprise, he found the idea of sending Doreen off with Snodgrass again unattended extremely uncomfortable. Even if he was willing to give Doreen the benefit of the doubt, and he didn't have much choice, he didn't trust Snodgrass as far as he could throw him. The guy was a snake; he knew that much. He would do anything he could to have Doreen work ALL of her magic on him. But Julian could no longer deny that if Doreen was going to do that with anyone, he wanted it to be with him and he was starting to want it bad.

After Lois and Mitch had safely dispensed with Clarissa, who was starting to come down some and was finally willing to be taken home, the group met for an early, pre-rush powwow.

Doreen was more than happy to be the center of attention as she gave her review of the 'sting operation,' as Tirana's ex-husband, Ted, had coined it. Mitch took her account at face value and praised her bravery. Lois, on the other hand, was not buying it one bit.

"I know what you're up to, Doreen. These blockheads might not see your game, but I'm all over it. You expect us to believe that Snodgrass's meeting with Fitz was all innocent and in the best interests of the plaintiffs?"

"The plaintiffs, who the hell are the plaintiffs, Lois? You're not making any sense, and of course you wouldn't believe anything I say because that's what you always do. Maybe it's a dyke thing. I sure wouldn't know. Would you know, Fellas?"

"A plaintiff is what we are, me and Julian, you dipstick. We are the ones suing Fitz. That makes us the plaintiffs, but I can see that I have to dumb down anything I say to you in order to make myself understood. I peg it at about third grade level English. You think you can handle third grade level English, Doreen?"

"I assure you I can handle anything you send my way, you old lezzie. Bring it on. Just cause I didn't get an A + in Volleyball doesn't mean I never learned to talk good and it doesn't mean you did neither."

"This is not helpful, Ladies. We are in the fight of our lives and our adversary is not each other but Fitz and very possibly our own legal representative. Lois, you got us into this whole thing and you said we were going to be rich and we've spent a pile of cash, your savings, my savings and, god bless him, Mitch's savings, which technically means Doreen's savings too. We stand to lose all of it if we don't stick together."

"Doreen's savings? That's a laugh riot, Jules. Doreen never saved so much as a Wheaties box top. Someone who has to steal glue from Hobby Lobby?"

"That's irrelevant and you know it. Now, Doreen here says that she thinks she can get more intel if she goes back in, but she needs updated equipment, an Apple Watch apparently, and I'm inclined to go ahead and get her one."

"For God's sake, how long have I been telling you I want an Apple Watch, but do I have one? No. And why don't I have one? Because I'm putting my money into this damn lawsuit where our attorney, and now even maybe Doreen here, are trying to double cross us. How about we get the watch for me and I go in?"

"No offense, Lo, but I don't think that would be as effective as my wife here being the one to go."

"I'm sorry, Lois. I'd be happy to give you the watch after I'm done with my important fact-gathering work with Snodgrass, but I'm afraid that any watch that would go around my teensy little wrist would never fit you. Just sayin."

"Lo, Doreen didn't mean that. Now, we all need to take a step back here. Look at it this way, the grill is killing it and I'm pretty sure you can afford your own Apple Watch now," Julian interjected.

"Hell, buy a couple, if you want. One for dress up and one for casual."

"How about one for casual and the other for car wreck, Lois? Since dressing up is so not your thing."

"Very funny, Doreen, maybe they make a trailer trash version or one especially for shoplifting glue sniffers."

"Neither of you are being helpful here."

"Helpful? Is that what you want, my friend? Helpful? What I think would be real helpful is if you got your head out of your pants and stopped siding with this low life whose working you like she works all men who are too stupid to know that's she's working them. And, by the way, she's not going to get away with working me. So, you decide whose side you're on in all this, Jules. Me, your supposed best friend, or this jamless pop tart."

"If I'm a pop tart, I guess that makes you a stack of pancakes with no syrup or any butter. Just plain."

"Enough! Maybe if you two would quit tearing one another down we could tackle the problems at hand as a strong unified team instead of a cat fighting sorority. I, myself, don't intend to take any side. What's good for each of us is good for the other so can we please start acting that way?"

"This bitch who came sashaying in here like she had any right, who turned Mitch's life upside down for the second time now and has brought nothing but trouble in her empty suitcase, is not part of any team I'll ever sign up for."

"Wouldn't you just love to be even considered for such a team like the one I'd be on. And that suitcase you're talking about, you owe me a new one."

CHAPTER
Eleven

As fortune would have it, Donna and Tibbets made their appearance before Lois could go on other than to advise Doreen that she'd be hearing from her later. The arrival of the two new emergency recruits necessitated bringing the focus back to the business. Lois shared the final tally from the day before and advised that Tirana was out stocking up on a huge order of food supplies in anticipation of an even bigger day ahead.

Fitz's younger brother's luxury discount mall was the big draw, apparently. The only restaurant on location was a Starbucks, and the nearest real food and drink were to be found at Barcus Bar and Grill. The hungry and thirsty shoppers, along with a growing number of regulars, locals and truckers, made the formerly gigantic parking lot seem small and inadequate.

This did not pass the attention of Fitz IV's younger, more clever, more acquisitive brother, and it kind of pissed him off. He didn't like the idea of some redneck townie profiting from his foresight and hard work. As soon as things settled a bit, he'd make an offer to this Mitch guy couldn't refuse. He would then tear the dump down and put up a respectable establishment to better cater to his clientele.

Nobody was surprised when Donna and Tibbets announced their engagement the week prior. Just as soon as Miss C turned eighteen and it was all cleared with her Dad and brothers, a daunting prospect much on Tibbet's mind, the invites would go out. Meanwhile, Donna thought it might be an opportune moment for her to drop out of Fitz Prep, which had become a joke and start working full time at the "BBG," as Tibbets had recently coined it.

Responsible mentor that he was, Julian strongly objected, but then somebody, Lois?, had the bright idea that he just tutor her so she could achieve her GED. Seeing how busy they were and knowing that they could really use all hands, Julian reluctantly agreed. He couldn't have known at the time that this prompted Lois to think about how much better it might be for her daughter, Shelley, to have hands-on schooling too. Julian was to have two new students, both of whom would present sizable challenges, each in her own unique way.

But this and other unfinished business was left on the table until after the noon rush, which seemed to continue on into dinner. By the time the last customer was seen out the door, a trucker named Orren who liked to do his eating late, his drinking later and then go sleep it all off in the cushy cab afforded by his semi, the crew was ready for their own cribs.

The next morning, Doreen didn't even have to ask for her coffee and jelly donut and Julian's attentiveness did not pass her notice.

"Well, if I wasn't just a little ol' country girl, I'd say that the distinguishable professor is paying a whole lot of attention to my needs these days."

"What? I was getting myself a cup of coffee and I saw you sitting here."

"You can't bullshit a bullshitter, Julie."

"Are you a bullshitter, Doreen? That's what Lois seems to think. She is dead certain you're double crossing us with Snodgrass and then there's this thing with Mitch, what's up with all that? You really want to stay married to Mitch?"

"Whoah, Mister, I guess you had your bowl of oats this morning. That's a lot of questions right there and, I might add, a little bit of a surprise coming from you."

Julian shrugged in response.

"I guess I'll just take those questions one at a time. Number one, I am so not double crossing you all. I could give Lois a bottle of Chanel No. Five still wrapped in its original wrapping and she would think I was trying to poison her or something, not that she'd wear any perfume. But I swear, Jules, if the damn wire hadn't been such crap and you had actually got to hear the whole conversation, you'd know that that's God's honest truth."

"Okay, I can accept that, see I'm inclined to believe you. I figured why else would you have gone to the trouble of telling us what went down at the Pancake Breakfast in the first place."

"Right? And as for me and Mitch."

"Mitch and me."

"What about Mitch and you?"

"No, not Mitch and me, you and Mitch, you just didn't say it properly."

"Oh geez, now you're gonna correct my English too?"

"Sorry, teacher's reflex."

"As I was saying, Mitch and me is between Mitch and me. I'm not at all sure we can make it work, but I do have feelings for the man. More like sister/brother feelings, if you have to know, but I don't see going and breaking his heart all over again for the second time."

"What if I told you, you wouldn't be breaking his heart if you just let him go."

"I'd suggest you help yourself to some more of that Koolaid you're drinking. I mean, really, look at him all skinny and bald and all. You think Mitch would ever in a gazillion years want to give this up? Did you not see how emotional he was when he first seen me coming home to him?"

Doreen reached across the table and lightly squeezed Julian's hand for emphasis. His metabolic reaction was such that he could no longer doubt that he had a major crush on this unlikeliest of love prospects.

"Speaking about which, what's with your divorce situation? You still have feelings for her? I heard she's a bitch. Anyways, Lois don't think much of her."

"I'm done. My attorney had the foresight to suggest I sign the divorce agreement before she got wind of the lawsuit, and Snodgrass insisted on it."

"See, he's not so bad as you all seem to think."

"We'll see."

Pouring drinks had become a rather satisfying occupation for Julian. His platform set up made accessing needed ingredients short work. He hadn't expected to ever find himself deriving pleasure and a sense of accomplishment from behind a bar. But he liked the physicality of it; so much more tangible than herding young, distracted minds toward an appreciation of great literature and very possibly more efficacious too.

His deftness at filling a half dozen unique cocktail orders in the time most people would take to pour a beer was athletic if you really thought about it. Bartending was Julian's new and so far best sport. People complimented him on this and did so often. The only compliments he'd ever gotten as a teacher were from Donna C., so that, in itself, was a huge difference.

He started to think that, if this was it, if they didn't win the lawsuit and he spent the rest of his working years right here where he found himself, that might actually be okay.

Lois was not as happy, he knew. She longed to have a whistle back between her teeth. If she could have had a whistle there at the bar and grill, she would have.

Tirana kept her from getting too far down in the dumps, and before too many more days, the paddle tennis court Mitch and Julian were having built for her out back would be ready. Maybe she could give lessons.

"We should gift wrap a whistle to tease the surprise," Julian thought.

This was good. Here at Mitch's Julian had found a career, a home and a family. The hippie commune of his upbringing had never been that. From the start, there was the apparent aberration of Julian's tendency toward the careful and conservative. His parents were so wrapped up in their drugs and their causes, they didn't know what to do with a little boy who insisted on keeping his shoes not just on but also polished, his hair cropped short and his bed made.

This kid of theirs hated the smell of weed, refused to eat kale, insisted on brushing his teeth after every meal and preferred eating those meals at the home of the Jehovah's Witnesses who lived down the street just outside the compound.

Granted, Lois, Tirana, Mitch, Doreen, Tibbets, Donna, Clarissa, Shelley, even Snodgrass, if he turned out to be legit, and Manny, who had proven to be a formidable valet, were the weirdest bunch of people ever to be assembled in one room, but they weren't idealogues. It was okay for everyone to be themselves.

Yup, this was good.

Clarissa showed up early as usual for the dinner shift. As she joined Julian behind the service bar, she greeted him like it was just another ordinary day. He wondered whether she had any recollection of their morning encounter.

"Well, don't you look handsome today, Julian. That a new tie or I just haven't seen it before?"

"I believe you saw it this morning, Clarissa."

"This morning?"

"Out in the field, out back."

"You sure about that?"

"Unless I was seeing things."

"Oh well, if you say so." Clarissa turned to the task of slicing lemons. "Mind if I help myself to a Maraschino?"

"You can have all the cherries you want. Oh, and I could use some more lemon wedges. It's been crazy busy again today."

"We are blessed; nuthin but to thank the lord for raining all this good fortune down upon us. You see this cherry stem? I'm going to take this cherry stem and tie it into a little knot in my mouth using no hands and only my tongue."

Julian watched Clarissa contort her mouth for half a minute and produce the promised knot.

"I didn't used to be able to do that. you know."

"What did you do? Practice for hours?"

"Nope, it just came to me out of the blue. Just one of the many ways my whole life seems to have changed for the better."

"What's your secret?"

"My secret, and it is confidential, Julian, is that whilst I was in the depths of a suicidal depression over the loss of my Mitch, my doctor prescribed a course of psychedelic mushrooms. Can you believe it? Me doing drugs of any kind, much less psychedelic? I have to tell you, I put up quite a resistance, a woman of my age doing drugs, but he convinced me that, if I couldn't get out of my funk what was the point of going on, and this stuff, he swore, could get me out of that funk. And, want to know something? He was right. I swear to you, Julian, I've never felt happier in my life, and the best part is I still love my Mitch, but I don't have to kill myself over it and also I can do this cherry thing now, which is really cool."

"Well, good for you, Clarissa, and full disclosure, my friend, I believe I witnessed one of your trips this morning."

"Oh, we don't call them 'trips,' Julie, we call them psychic journeys."

"Okay, that then."

"This doesn't surprise me. I've been known to turn up in all sorts of places when I'm under the influence. Lucky you, though, because my doctor thinks it is mission accomplished time. No need to do any more of the tripping of the light fandango, if you know what I mean. I'm cured!"

"Well, that's just great. Whatever it takes. And stopping at the right time is good too. As we've gone over in session, my parents and their friends never did stop."

"Oh yes, that's right. I forgot how anti-drug you are, but everything in moderation as they say, even psilocybin as it turns out. Now, this is just between you and me, huh? Let me go get you some more of those lemons."

CHAPTER
Twelve

Manny and his crew put the finishing touches on Lois's paddle tennis court just in time for her birthday and while Tirana kept her occupied shopping for an Apple Watch at the mall. When the two returned, it was to a surprise party attended by all the crew: Lois's ex, Ronny, and their daughter, Shelley, Manny, Clarissa, the kids as she called Tibbets and Donna and, of course, Julian, Mitch and Tirana's ex, Ted. One big happy family. As a rule, Lois was not so big on birthdays, insisting that they just made her feel old and, even worse, made her feel sentimental. Though her loved ones knew this, they weren't deterred and all were relieved to see her reclaim her joie de vivre, so to speak, once she'd recovered from the "SURPRISE!"

All seemed to be enjoying themselves, apart from a brief moment of concern when Ronny and Ted's dates started dancing together to Mitch's favorite tune, 'Me and Mrs. Jones.'

As Lois tore through the thoughtful gifts, gloves, cologne (men's), a woolen scarf, a book about the academy awards, etc., only the whistle made her pause. She immediately put it around her neck and gave it a full throated test blow enough to almost knock the celebrants off their seats. Everyone cheered. Julian tapped his glass with a spoon to signal the group to quiet down and let him speak.

"Lo, we're all here to celebrate your special day and to wish you many more to come. You may be asking yourself, why a whistle? Well, it's a good question. One for which the answer will require a little journey."

"You kidding me, Jules? You think I'm going anywhere? I've been out all day and you all are having this party for me whether I wanted a party or not. So I'm here trying to make the best of it and I don't need a reason to have a whistle. I'm used to a whistle. I've had a whistle half my life. Me and my whistle are not going anywhere."

"Ahhh, ok, how about just out back behind the kitchen? You won't regret it I promise."

"Tirana, do I need to be doing this? Is there any reason you can think of why I need to leave now? I got my beer and I'm assuming there's going to be some cake and all."

"I think it's OK, doll. You just try and have a little faith now. Maybe you'll be pleasantly surprised."

"Can I bring my beer?"

"Yes" was the chorus from the assembled co-conspirators and off they went.

It was the closest that any of them had seen Lois come to shedding a tear, and from the moment she took the court, the party remained outside for the rest of the afternoon. Beer and cake were delivered and consumed. Lois didn't stop until she'd challenged and annihilated everyone with the exception of Doreen, who was conveniently having lunch with Snodgrass and Mitch who claimed to be strictly an indoor sports man.

The only opponent to give her any kind of run for her money was sporty Manny, who was unwittingly sealing his fate to spend what would be years of his life on the other side of a net from Lois.

As the party wound down and most took their leave, Lois sat in a booth with Tirana, Shelley, Tibbets and Donna, impatiently trying to master her Apple Watch, which she was beginning to think had been a frivolous purchase.

Mitch and Julian sat outside engaging in a bit of boys' talk.

"You said you like indoor sports, you mean darts?"

"No, Jule, I'm a pool man."

"Pool, huh?"

"Since I was no bigger than you, eleven, twelve years old."

"Okay, okay, I get it. What you're saying is I'm the size of a twelve year old. Thanks, pal; thanks for pointing that out."

"Oh, geez, Julian, I'm sorry, I wasn't thinking. Got my mind all messed up seeing Clarissa like that today."

"I know you didn't mean it, Mitch, of course you didn't, but tell me. What's got you so wound up?"

"Like I said, it's the Clarissa thing. She looked so pretty and she's taking this so well now and I guess maybe it's my turn to fall apart. I miss her so much. I really, really do."

"You don't have to be doing this. Doreen left you. And if that lowlife she took off with hadn't lost all the money and she hadn't seen that article that made it look like you were doing so well, she wouldn't have come back here at all. So you being so loyal to her is pretty one-sided from what I can tell."

"Maybe you're right. Maybe I'm just an old fool."

Just then, a silver Chevy Camaro pulled into the parking lot and screeched to a dusty stop. The top was down so that it wasn't difficult to spot Snodgrass behind the wheel and Doreen settled in next to him. He said something and Doreen howled with laughter.

Julian turned to Mitch.

"Think about it, okay? Just think about it."

Snodgrass turned off the engine and stepped around the car to get the door for his date. She placed her hand on his forearm and lifted herself up with a huge shopping bag in hand.

As the two walked toward the stoop where Julian and Mitch sat, the former noticed that she was wearing a whole new outfit from the one she had left in that morning. The shopping bag said "GUESS."

"Looks like someone's been doing some shopping," Julian said trying to manage his resentment to a deniable tinge.

"Well, I never thought you'd notice, Professor. Tee-hee. Mr. Snodgrass, Esquire, as I understand, was not only kind enough to take me to lunch, but we popped into the high-end mall just for curiosity sake and then I saw there was a Guess store in there and I just cannot resist Guess, my favorite designer since I was knee high to a grasshopper, and oh well, there were all kinds of bargains in there at seventy percent off so what girl can resist that?"

Julian noted that Doreen was more breathless than ever and wondered whether it was her date, the clothes or the fact that she knew she was treading on thin ice.

"I wanted to get her a little something. She works so hard," Snodgrass threw in.

"You bought the clothes?" Mitch asked as he stood up to tower over the lawyer.

"Yeah, no big deal. I was more than happy to do it, Mitch."

Mitch took a wad of cash out of his back pocket and started to peel off twenties.

"What do I owe you? Hundred bucks cover it?"

"No, keep your money, Mitch; it was nothing. No harm done, just a spontaneous thing since we were checking out the mall."

"You put that money away right now, Mitchy. I used my own money to buy these things."

As she said this, she winked at Julian as if he would have her back in this.

"Golly, you have a jealous streak. Me and Mr. Snodgrass here just spent an innocent afternoon as friends, and me steering clear of the lesbian birthday celebration, by the way. We mostly just were discussing your all's case and I think you'll like hearing what he had to tell me. So everybody just calm down and I'm going to go use the little girl's room and you boys find a spot and pour yourselves a drink. I'll take the usual if anyone is asking."

Lois's Apple Watch was back in the box she bought it in while she thought about whether it was too "techno" to be worth her bother. The stragglers were gathering their things and preparing to go.

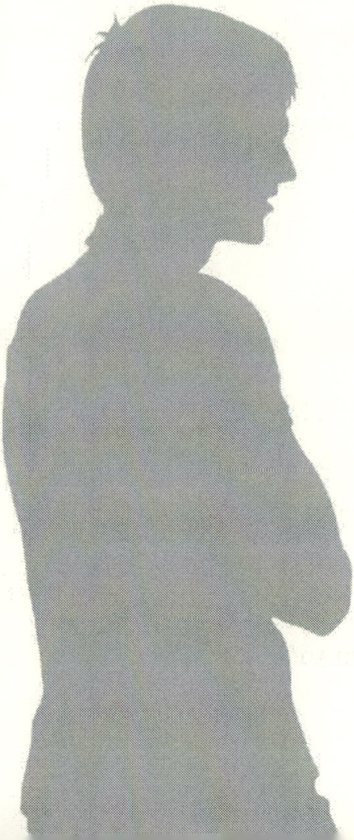

CHAPTER Thirteen

Nobody expected to hear what they heard from Snodgrass and, coming on the heels of a big day of partying, it was almost more than any of them could take.

"Here's the dealio, kids. I'm in a position to make all of you very, very, very rich."

"Are they going to settle? Is that what this is?" Lois wanted to know.

"Not technically, but wait, wait, hear me out. So, as Doreen here can tell you, Fitz cornered me at the pancake breakfast down at the firehouse and asked me to come out to his car. I've been in this business long enough, I can tell you, to know when to say 'yes' to an invitation like that and, just as I suspected, the guy was trying to buy me off, sell you all down the river."

"That weasel, I knew it, I knew he was going to try to pull something," Julian said after pounding the table with his fist.

"Now, settle down there, Tiger. It's all for the best. See, I taped the guy on my trusty Apple Watch. So I've got him, right to nines, but I have to play along and let him think I'm really considering his offer, which, by the way, was for half a million bucks, which he does not have cash on hand, of this I'm sure."

"So what did you say?"

"I said I'd think about it and get back to him."

"But he could raise that kind of money if he had to, so I don't get it. You telling us we got ourselves an honest lawyer?" Lois asked.

"Not an honest lawyer, Lois, a smart lawyer."

"Really a genius lawyer if you have to know, Lois," Doreen piped in.

"You keep out of this. This has nothing to do with you."

"Oh so only when I was the one to tell you about seeing Marty and Fitz meeting up..."

"Wait, who's Marty?"

"Marty is Snodgrass, Mitchy."

"Okay, can I go on?"

"Go on, Snodgrass or maybe I should call you Marty like your new best friend over here."

"Lois, you can pretty much call me whatever you want, just let me finish talking first, okay? So, anyway, I happen to know a thing or two about old man Fitzgerald. A: That he's a stickler for the family reputation. It's all got to be on the up and up, everything by the books and all that. B: He has a whole lot more money than his Headmaster loser of a son. So, I set up a meeting and advised him not to have his namesake in attendance. When I got there, it was just him and the younger son, the successful one. I told them about the tape and then I played them the tape. Then, before the old man could recover his composure, to put it mildly, I informed him, in so many words and as diplomatically as possible, that I was prepared to go public with it. 'Of course, we can settle this whole thing in a much less slanderous fashion,' I told him. And when he asked what that would look like, I suggested we settle the lawsuit for a commensurate amount. He then asked me what exactly did that mean, a commensurate amount, I told him twenty million."

"Twenty million, Jesus! What did he say to that?"

"I can't repeat what he said in polite company, Julian. Suffice it to say he was a very, very unhappy camper at that point. He told me to get the hell out of his office and never darken his doorway again. I just told him, 'Okay, I'm leaving, but you've got twenty-four hours to think about it and you better take me seriously when I say I'm locked and loaded.'"

"When was this?" Julian asked.

"This was Saturday."

"So, Sunday came and almost went and I was beginning to think the old miser was calling my bluff. To be honest, I briefly considered taking another look at Fitz the IV offer, figuring that might be better than nothing."

"You did what?" Lois asked.

"Sorry, but let's be real, Lois, I am a lawyer and when I looked at the odds of us successfully going up against the Fitzgeralds in a court of law presided over by a judge who they bought and paid for, I figured I better hedge my bets."

"Are you telling me we weren't going to win after all? Is that what you're saying? All that talk about a strong case, that was all just bullshit to get our hard earned money?" Lois clenched her fists and almost reached for her whistle.

"That's pretty much what I'm saying. But hold on, it all worked out for the best. Now, quit interrupting me so I can give you the good news. It was ten minutes to three in the afternoon and I was sitting in my office and the phone rang. And bingo, it was old man Fitz telling me to be at his place in an hour. You can bet I showed up right on time. It was him and the younger son again and I almost fell out of my chair when they told me they'd come up with a way to work things out. So, here's the deal. First and foremost, we get the twenty million."

Snodgrass paused to take in the expressions of shock and triumph registering on the faces of his clients.

"What's the catch? Got to be some kind of catch," the ever skeptical Lois observed.

"Well, there is a catch, but not much of one if you add it all up. They want a couple of little things in return for making us all rich. First, we have to make it look like a business transaction rather than a settlement. We have to withdraw the suit so it doesn't appear that the Fitz's capitulated. Second, by a stroke of luck, the younger Fitz, the one who built the outlets and has a clue about how to make money has an interest in purchasing this property and the business. For our part, and so they have an insurance policy against us, we cook the books majorly, thereby documenting financial fraud that they can hold as a deterrent against anyone ever talking and against that tape of Fitz IV ever coming out in public. It's a no brainer."

"Hold on there, Mr. Snodgrass, you telling us that we have to sell the Barcus as part of this arrangement here?"

"Yes, I am telling you that, Mitch. I'm telling you you're going to sell this place for forty times it's real commercial value and never have to work a day again in your life."

"But what if I don't want to sell?"

"What are you talking about, man? Look at this place. You really willing to give up twenty million cash for this? I'm sure your partners here would not like to pass up the opportunity of a lifetime to hang on to a losing proposition."

"How you calling this a losing proposition? Business has never been better."

"It's good now, but supposing, and this is a hypothetical, but a fairly viable one, supposing young Fitz decides to invest a fraction of that twenty million, you're talking about saving him and his daddy in a world class establishment right across the road. There's a guy who owns that property who I'm sure would be more than happy to sell for what, a couple hundred thousand bucks? Did you not hear me? I said twenty million dollars, twenty million! Lois? Julian? I already know what Doreen thinks."

"Doreen is not part of this decision," Lois said. "And I can tell you that she might think she gets half of what Mitch gets, but I happen to know that the law, unlike the lawyer, is not on her side."

"Very funny, Lois. So funny I forgot to laugh out loud. Did you forget to laugh out loud too Marty?"

"You think I'm joking, Doreen? Let me ask you, where did you first meet Mitch?"

"What? Here at the bar."

"And who owned that bar already when you met him?"

"You know Mitch owned it, Lois, because he inherited it from his daddy. Spit it out, Lois, what are you trying to say."

"What I'm not even trying to say but actually really saying, little Miss, is that you have no stake in whatever Mitch gets for this here property because he already owned it long before he met you and for sure before he made the mistake of making you his wife."

"Well, I never heard such hogwash in my life, Lois, and I've heard a whole lot of hogwash, especially from one overweight Lesbo I've had the unpleasure of knowing. Marty, tell Lois here that she better stick with bodily functions instead of trying to tell us what the law says."

"Uh, I hate to say this, but she actually has a point, Doreen. If we handle this as proposed and I don't see any other option, then all the money would technically be Mitch's, which isn't to say he couldn't share some with you, but that'd be up to him."

It was fortuitous that Doreen was wearing her brand new outfit from the Guess outlet or there would have been an all out drag down for sure. Rather than fight, her first instinct, she implored Mitchy to set the record straight in her favor and getting no response at all, slapped him across the face, referred to her husband as the cadaver she had wasted the prime of her youth sleeping next to, released a torrent of tears and ran out the front door. But not before castigating Snodgrass for being either a liar or a not genius at all lawyer and that he could take his pick.

"Hey, hey, what about the nice things I bought you and the lunch?"

"So you did buy her those clothes," Mitch said as he began to stand up out of his seat.

Julian put his hand on Mitch's arms gently encouraging the big guy to just sit back down. He politely thanked Snodgrass for his service and asked that he leave the three of them some privacy to discuss the matter among themselves.

Snodgrass admonished them not to take too long and not to be foolish. He repeated the number, twenty million, several times over before taking his leave. It turned out that, despite the impressive number and the math that indicated that each of them stood to pocket over three million in cold hard cash, the sentimentality that made Mitch hesitate was not exclusive to him.

Julian reflected back on his ridiculously untethered days in the commune and the very polite, yet not particularly warm, experience afforded by his maternal grandparents. Nothing had ever come close to the sense of family he experienced here with his nutty friends and partners at Barcus Bar and Grill. Lois kept reflecting on all the good times spent on her paddle tennis court. Yes, she'd be in a position to build a new paddle tennis court, or any kind of court she wanted for that matter, but it wouldn't be THE paddle tennis court and Tirana wouldn't be glancing out at her from the kitchen window, and what about Manny? Who would be her go-to opponent if it wasn't Manny?

"What you thinking, Lo?" Julian broke the silence.

"Oh, nuthin', my paddle tennis court if you have to know."

"Mitch?"

"A couple of things, my dad and what my wife just said about me. Look, guys, I'm not going to stand in your way here. We're looking at more money than any of us is probably going to see in a lifetime."

"You're a good man, Mitch O'Gorman. You too, Jules. What do you say we sleep on it; maybe give it a week. Okay?"

"I'm a little worried about if we turn this down and Fitz, the younger whatever his name is, opens up a fancy place across the street and we go back to the days of just me behind the bar and you two sitting on the other side and the parking lot empty and not having any work for the kids or Tirana or her kitchen staff or even Clarissa, if she even had any feelings left for me by that point."

"Which she would, Mitch. You've got to learn the difference between a woman who's in for the thick and thin and one who's just in it for whatever blood she can suck out of you. You need me to tell you which one is which?"

"No, Lo."

"I didn't think so. And don't worry about business. We have a good thing going here and I'll die keeping it going if those fat cats try to muscle in on our success. So, just go think about what you need to think about and we'll talk in a couple of days. Like a wise man said, 'worrying is just the illusion of control.'"

"Amen to that, my friend."

Lois did something she had never done before. She apologized for dragging Julian and Mitch into a case which she had believed was a sure fire winner for them. Upon this, Mitch, of all people, executed a first of his own and extended his arms to his friends.

Julian was the first to see that Mitch was offering a hug. Lois needed a minute to figure it out and then the three partners had their first, and probably last, group hug. This is what young Tibbets witnessed when he came in the door.

"Yo, excuse me, this a bad time?"

The partners in hug quickly shoved off one another as if the last man hugging would take the entire brunt of Tibbets mockery. But Tibbets didn't mock. He actually had been prepared to join in the hug. He, for one, loved group hugs and he loved all three of the people he found group hugging.

"Just having a moment. No big deal, Tibbets," Lois assured him.

"No, it was nice, Lois. It's nice to know that grownups aren't afraid to show that they love one another."

"Well I don't know if I'd go that far, kid."

"It's all good, Lois. I get it. I know how you guys feel about each other. As Donna would say, 'it's a beautiful something else,' by which she means it's a beautiful thing. Anyway, she's waiting in the car while I grab Julian."

"Grab me? For what?"

"Remember you promised to come ice skating with us up at Laurel Lake; Donna's waiting in the car and she went all the way home to get her brother's old skates for you. She's super excited."

"Oh, geez, I totally forgot. It's been a pretty intense day, kid."

"No worries, we can wait, but better hurry it up before the sun goes down."

Julian looked to his two partners and noted their silent nods of encouragement. What harm could it do to go clear his head and have a little fun. Barcus would love it too.

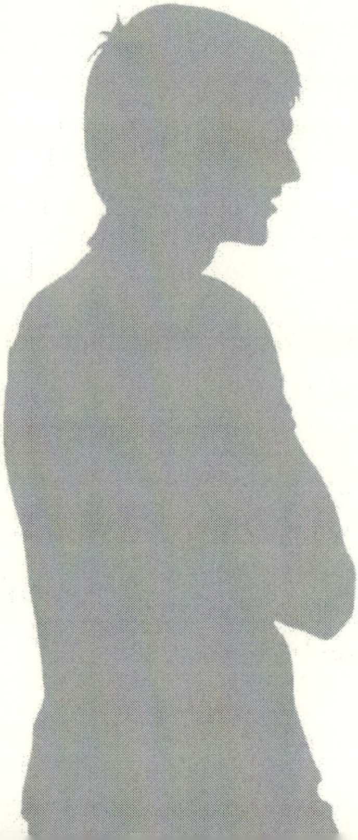

CHAPTER Fourteen

When they'd driven a few miles, Tibbets zoomed past a lone person hobbling down the side of the road. He checked her out in the rearview mirror and instinctively hit the brakes.

"It's Doreen," he said, as he turned to look over his shoulder and set the car in reverse.

Doreen was beyond happy to see her friends. She climbed in the back seat with Julian and Barcus and rather rudely clambered over the dog to sit snuggly against his master.

"Leave it to a real gentleman to come along and rescue a frozen little lady from being picked up by who knows what and getting kidnapped or put in the sex trade or something. Why can't all men be like my professor, I'd like to ask?"

Just a day earlier, Julian would have lapped up this flirtation, but something had come disconnected in him when he saw how Doreen treated Mitch and even Snodgrass.

"She's just a user," he thought and had to wonder why he hadn't seen it before. "Lois had been right dammit; she'd been right all along."

Julian could see exactly what Doreen's game plan was. Now that she couldn't count on divorce law as she'd thought, Mitch was no longer of any use to her, she'd alienated Snodgrass for good and went on to tell them about the way he worried over the price of things at a discount outlet and had taken her to half price happy hour at The Golden Corral in Stockbridge after promising her a fancy restaurant. It was clear. Julian was her last best chance at getting her hands on any real money in her present situation and she was going all out to make a play for him.

"Ice skating? I've always wanted to ice skate ever since I was just a wee little bit growing up in the panhandle, dreaming about snow and ice skating, but mostly ice skating."

The place was quiet and nearly empty, apart from a group of kids at the far end riding their toboggan down a swath in the pine trees and out onto the icy surface of the pond.

Since Doreen didn't have skates or even flat shoes, she was agreeable to waiting to borrow Donna's after a little bit. As Donna and Tibbets glided off arm in arm, their woolen scarves flowing out behind them, their mittens and skates and slightly bent stance was as Currier and Ives as anything Julian had ever seen in real life. He stood up to catch up with them, but Doreen literally pulled him back down to sit on the log they shared and admonished him not to leave a little lady all by her lonesome or some such nonsense. Barcus who clearly and uncharacteristically found Doreen to be an, at best, negligible human bounded off to check out the tobogganers.

Julian was not happy to have to give up his toasty down jacket with the faux fur lined hood to Doreen who was, as usual, completely inappropriately dressed. He was even less happy to see that, petite as she was, the jacket fit her like a glove. When she cracked a joke about them being able to share their wardrobes, he very nearly gave her a piece of his mind.

Donna and Tibbets shooshed to an impressive stop right in front of them. Their cheeks were rosy and steam came puffing out of their smiling mouths. Donna helped Doreen get into the skates and took her Apple Watch and rhinestone earrings for safekeeping and then it was on Julian to steer her across the ice. This turned out to be trickier than it appeared.

Doreen, the 'dancer' seemed incapable of even standing still on her blades, much less gliding gracefully across the ice as she had envisioned. Julian's experience with skating had been up in Canada as a kid when he found his mother's strap-on double metal blades from the box of belongings her parents had long since unburdened themselves of. If he could skate on those, he could skate on anything, he thought. His low center of gravity helped to seal the deal and he found himself fairly steady, which was good. But not steady enough to balance himself and the weight of a flailing partner. Every time she fell down, she dragged Julian with her.

Tibbets being the sort of young man he was, came to the rescue and took hold of Doreen's other side. The two men proceeded to more or less drag her along between them, pausing every ten feet or so to stabilize her. Doreen thought this was all too fun. She was nice and warm in Julian's coat and all of the exertion was on the part of her two swains. Julian, who was freezing his ass off, was not amused. And so they were straggling along, a not universally happy trio when out of the corner of his eye, Tibbets saw the toboggan speeding toward them at warp speed.

"Watch out," he screamed as he and Julian tried to push Doreen out of the way and were barely able to then position themselves safely.

The trouble was that they pushed Doreen too far out of the way and onto the thinner ice for which a makeshift barrier of road cones had been set up by a caring citizen. Doreen blew through the barrier, screeching all the way and then disappeared with a crash of ice and splash of water.

Julian told Tibbets to go call for help and he slid down on the ice and started to crawl to the site of Doreen's disappearance.

He was relieved to see her head bob up and to hear her familiar screaming. He traversed the thin ice just as far as he dared, grabbed a stick and stretched absolutely as far as he could stretch, which was just inches shy of Doreen's cold, grasping hand.

"Further, come further, you little chicken shit; if you let me die here in this goddamn, freezing ass shithole, I'm gonna... can't breathe."

Tibbets returned with Donna, a rope and, of course, his camera. He tossed Julian the rope. Julian managed to feed the rope to Doreen and he told the toboggan kids to form a human chain and grab his feet and pull and so, with quick thinking and Herculean effort, if not human length, he saved the fairy princess who, in truth, in action and in word, was more like the wicked witch.

Doreen wasn't hot, but she was a mess. The minute she was able to speak again, she told Tibbets he would publish those pictures over her dead body. Tibbets just told her he'd take it under advisement and winked at his girlfriend, chancing the possibility that she would wink back and so she did.

When Doreen tried to cuddle up to Julian in the back seat as if everything was fine, he politely scooted away.

When she moved closer he said, "Please, no, you're all wet."

"Well, so much for you being a gentleman and even if you were, it wouldn't be a man-sized gentleman anyways."

"Whatever," Julian shrugged.

None of the group was the least bit surprised, or in any way disappointed ,to see Doreen, cleaned up and back in her old clothes, pulling her one wheeled American Tourister across the restaurant floor. She had managed to hit Mitch up for a couple hundred bucks and would be taking a Greyhound back down to where it never snowed. The only good thing that had come out of her months here in the inhospitable North was that Snodgrass, for the one-time gift of ALL of Doreen's magic, had expunged her record.

This would prove imperative when she sought employment at Disney World. Being Snow White wasn't very lucrative, but the hours were good and it was as close as she would ever come to being in showbiz so she was content. As her dwarves gathered around her, she couldn't help but think with fondness about Julian. Having been chastened to a degree by her experiences and a bus ride, glue sniffing binge that left her in very poor shape, she became a tea-totaller and began to truly believe that she really was Snow White.

"When you gonna take off that damn costume?" her mama would ask between puffs of her Marlboro Reds and slugs out of her Gordon's Vodka bottle.

The very night that Doreen left, Clarissa was back with her Mitch. He was excited to show her how Manny had fixed up the old pool table and hoped she'd be less dismissive of it than Doreen had been. She was.

Donna and Tibbets popped in to check on the skating accident victim and were blown away to find her gone.

"Who just gets up and goes away after a situation like the one that happened to her?" Donna asked. "And, hey, in case anybody is asking, I've got her Apple Watch and these earrings."

"Her clearing out of here was the best birthday gift I could have asked for," Lois said.

"And, speaking of happy birthday presents, how about, if you still want to return your Apple Watch that you paid so much money for, Miss Lois, and get a free one to keep instead? You take this?"

"Donna, I think you're a whole lot more clever than people give you credit for."

"That's nice of you. Thanks a bundle, Miss Lois. Here, ya go and happy birthday many times over as they say."

Throughout the busy week ahead, nobody even mentioned Snodgrass or his proposal. Of course, he called every day, but every day he got the same answer. Meanwhile, as requested, Shelley, who was something of a math whiz, was running some numbers. Each of the partners secretly hoped that she could tell them that, over a given period of time, they could make up the amount they were walking away from if, in fact, they walked away. She could not.

The story that Tibbets wrote about the skating incident and Julian's heroic actions was accompanied by dramatic photos, none of which would have been sanctioned by Doreen. They cast Julian in a favorable light though, that was for sure, and many were the congratulations and pats on the back he received for this for years to come. The person least positively impressed was Fitz IV, who was seething with jealousy and righteous umbrage having been severely chastised by his domineering father. He had no one better to blame than one Julian Dickerson and blame him he did.

Donna and Shelley proved to be earnest, if not conventional students. Julian found he enjoyed this more casual, less cumbersome way of teaching. He liked dabbling in all the many different subjects that had previously been outside of his purview. He felt that he had two of the sweetest kids to guide along the path of higher learning and they clearly adored him; especially Shelley who took every chance to remind him that she was no longer a 'kid.'

Julian had to agree and to admit that Shelley's brief lessons in feminine tricks of the trade, kindly provided by the otherwise useless Doreen, had made him see his student in a different light. But such reflections were fleeting. Julian found he had enough on his mind just thinking about the large fortune within his reach and what he would have to sacrifice to grab hold of it.

When the partners convened to get Shelley's sobering assessment that it would take quite a few years and a Spartan budget and work ethic to match for them to get anywhere close to the riches being proffered, the three registered the disappointment equally.

Their reaction in itself was telling, but not conclusive. Since Snodgrass had been badgering them daily, they all decided to put him off until after the holidays. They agreed to explain that they were just too busy to give it the attention needed and, in this, they were absolutely prescient. The bar and grill operated at full capacity as shoppers poured in to fortify themselves for the mad purchasing ahead or to console themselves after having done this and thereby dropped a fortune.

Donna and Shelley decorated the place in a charming traditional holiday fashion and Clarissa added some flair with her unicorns and dream catchers, insisting that decorations were decorations and, this way, there'd be something for everyone, even the nonbelievers, "bless their souls."

It was with the greatest relief that they finally closed shop on Christmas day and joined with all of their friends in a celebration and exchange of presents of their own.

Julian got everyone a gift card to CVS, a choice he regretted when he opened the more personal selections his friends had made for him. In his defense, Christmas had never been celebrated at the commune and the couple of such holidays he spent with his grandparents were relatively Spartan.

He was touched by the custom tailored barmans apron from Mitch and Clarissa, the pocketknife from Lois and even the Himalayan salt lamp from Donna and Tibbets, but nothing topped the first edition of The Little Prince that Shelley had found and paid a small fortune for.

Her card read, 'You might be little, but you are a prince.'

Julian thanked her and said that he had never read it.

"It's a children's book," she said. "But everyone should read it and especially you."

When Shelley left that night to go to Catamount to ski with her dad for a few days, Julian walked her to the door. She looked him in the eyes and pointed to the mistle-toe above their heads and bent down to kiss him on the lips.

Julian was in shock. He just stood there watching her go out the door and greet her dad. He'd been aware that, possibly,

Shelley had developed a bit of a teacher's crush, but he never imagined it might really mean something to her, or to him for that matter. The kiss was a really good kiss. What would Lois say? Lois would kill him.

Over the next few days, Julian couldn't get Shelley and her kiss out of his mind, but this dreamy reflection was inevitably followed by an unpleasant one of Lois and her fist.

Not knowing where else to turn, he brought the situation up with Clarissa. While Shelley had been there working with them, she had been seeing Clarissa about her bouts with depression.

"Well, my friend," Clarissa began. "Can I tell you that this doesn't really surprise me? As you know, I've been seeing Shelley and I take patient/doctor confidentiality very seriously. But I'm just saying, I'm not surprised; nothing more, nothing less."

"I understand you. Maybe you can tell me how you think Lois would respond to me having anything to do on an intimate level with her daughter."

"Not kindly, I'm afraid. No, not kindly at all."

"That's what I thought."

"But, Julian, may I ask you what your feelings are in all this?"

"I don't even know, to be honest, Clarissa. I'd say I'm so worried about how Lois might react that I can't think for myself."

"Well, you're just going to have to find that inner voice we've talked about, my friend; and, when you find it, I very much suggest you listen to it. Life is short, Julie, even shorter..."

Julian raised his hand to prevent Clarissa from completing her thought.

"I hear you." He said. "I hear you."

Shelley returned from her ski vacation looking fit, healthy, happy and more attractive than ever. Julian could no longer assure himself that he had any control over his feelings. He noticed too that Shelley's affection was much more obvious when her mother wasn't nearby. He invited Shelley to accompany him and Barcus and Sonia, who now acted more like a dog than a cat, much to Julian's preference, on one of their morning hikes.

The minute they had walked through mother nature's front door and found themselves in a world of towering and fragrant pines, Shelley went to grab Julian's hand. He held onto hers for a second and then restored it back to her.

"Look," he said. "Shelley, we need to talk."

"Oh no, please, Julian."

"No, listen," he said. "It's not that I don't have feelings for you. I can't tell you that, in all honesty. But there are several factors, which make me uncomfortable. The age difference for one."

"Eleven years? My father is fourteen years older than my mom."

"Well, your mom is another reason. Your mom is my best friend I guess you could say and you know as well as I do that she would not take this in a good way, you and me getting together. The third thing is that I'm your teacher and, as such, you may look up to me so that your feelings might be unduly influenced."

"Ya, and what about the fourth thing, Julian, let's not forget that."

"What fourth thing, what do you mean?"

"You know, the fourth thing, the fact that why would anyone want to get involved with a manic depressive who doesn't even afford the payback of ever being manic and is only ever depressive, that fourth thing."

"No, of course not, that has nothing to do with it."

"That's what they all say."

With that, Shelley turned around and ran out of the woods. Julian was grateful she hadn't chosen to run in the other direction at least. His two companions were not happy that rather than the usual brisk hike they were getting a prolonged stand still.

In response to their relentless protests, Julian continued on the trail carrying the weights of a heavy heart and a guilty conscience.

"Some pole vaulter, you are," he said to himself.

For the rest of the day, Shelley avoided not just Julian, but everyone. When she emerged from her session with Clarissa, she was wearing dark glasses. Julian was well aware that this was to hide the evidence of red and swollen eyes. He felt like such a heel and was stuck with doubt over whether he had done the right thing.

He wanted to wrap her in his arms and assure her that everything would be alright and that he really had come to care for her deeply and that they would face Lois together, but he did not.

With the holidays behind them and Snodgrass breathing down their necks, the partners assembled to find a consensus.

Clarissa was in attendance with Shelley's spreadsheets and Mitch introduced a piece of news that could be helpful.

"Clarissa has something to tell us."

"No, you tell them, Mitch."

"Okay, I'll go first. My clever girl here had expressed to me, after we all met over the numbers Shelley had come up with, that all our calculations aside, the biggest threat to turning down the offer and keeping our place would be if Junior bought the lot across the street and took our business out from under us. So I thought about it and I remember meeting the guy who owns that land and Clarissa found him on the internet. So, I went ahead and called him and I got his son, who told me his pop had passed on. I told him how sorry I was and he asked if there was something he could help me with. Bottom line, he quoted me two thousand bucks an acre if we bought all eighty-two and three thousand if we bought a smaller amount."

"We have fifteen thousand, which was meant for the new roof," Clarissa chimed in.

"If we use that to buy the road front part of the property across the way, see, if we can get him to agree to four acres for ten thousand, we don't have to worry about the Fitzgerald's putting up a restaurant or anything else over there."

Lois shook her head. "I don't know, I don't know. I should just sit this one out and leave it up to you," she said. "I'm the one who got us into this mess in the first place."

"Lo, it's okay. Your opinion is just as important as anyone's. But I have to say, I'm very nervous about spending even more money than we already have on this thing. I mean, it sounds good, but that roof is not in great shape and what about what we still owe to Snodgrass? What happens with that?"

"What happens with that, Jule, I'll tell you what happens with that, nothing, bubkas, de nada, not one red cent. And if the only thing I do is not pay his bill, he's going to consider himself lucky."

"Okay, so what does everybody think?" Clarissa asked.

The partners sat in silence until Julian asked Lois what time it was.

"Hell, I know."

"Where's your new fancy watch?"

"Gave it to my kid."

More time passed with no one saying a word. Tirana broke the verbal impasse when she emerged from the kitchen asking anyone if they'd seen her potato masher. The joyless group answer was "No."

As opening time approached and no decision had been made and/or voiced, a plan was agreed to reconvene that evening. It turned out to be a slow day, the first in a long time. This anomaly weighed on the three deciders.

Shelley didn't show up at the appointed time for homeschooling. It was just Donna and Julian, and they were both concerned.

"Well, cheer up, Mr. D, maybe she just isn't here because of a cold or headache or something or maybe it's her, you know, time of the month, which I kind of wish it was mine, but if I'm expecting something, it's probably not my period."

"What? What are you saying, Donna?"

"What I'm saying, Mr. D, is that I'm pretty sure that there's a little Tibbets or a little Donna or a little Tibbets and Donna making me want to throw up in the morning, but also making me very excited and kind of nervous."

"Oh, geez. What's your dad going to think?"

"My dad is why the kind-of-nervous comes into it. My dad thinks I'm the only good and responsible one in his whole family since my brothers are such meat heads and my mom, well, you know."

"I don't know what to say."

"For one, congratulations would be nice, and if maybe you could go with Tibbets as a respectable teacher of mine and tell my dad about my boyfriend's hard work and niceness...."

"I guess; could we bring Lois?"

"Of course, Mr. D, of course we can, what were you thinking?"

That night as the partners and Clarissa reconvened, the subject of whether or not to take Snodgrass' offer was pushed to the back of the line behind Donna and Shelley.

"I told her, you're coming, Lo."

"Well thanks for volunteering me. I guess now I'm supposed to be you and Tibbet's bodyguard or something. What happened to James Bond 007, Mr. Bigstuff?"

"I just think there's strength in numbers."

"I'll tell you where there's strength, see this? This is where all the strength in this particular group of numbers is," Lois presented her bicep.

"Whatever. We're going; we're doing it for those sweet kids and that's the end of it."

"Yes, sir, whatever you say, sir," Lois saluted.

"In the meantime, I'm willing to help Donna, but what am I supposed to do about my own daughter? It's happening again and here she'd been so good for so many months. You see the signs, Clarissa? What are we supposed to do; you're the expert."

"Well, Lois, I have your daughter's permission to tell you that we discussed the measured application of psilocybin, which I personally had so much success with and I highly recommend in Shelley's case."

"My daughter on drugs? I think you still might be high yourself, Clarissa."

"She is very much interested in giving it a try. She believes that she's been through every other conceivable treatment and feels that it could only help."

"Maybe you should consider it, Lo, she is twenty-two years old, doesn't that mean she doesn't technically need parental consent? Look how it helped Clarissa. So it's a drug, she wouldn't be abusing it. What's the big deal?"

Julian surprised himself with the force of the stand he was taking and imagined, correctly, that he was desperate to see Shelley back to normal and assuage his own guilt.

"I'll tell you what, my little, big mouthed friend, you take a trip on that damn stuff and, if you come out good, maybe I'll let Shelley give it a try."

"What? Are you out of your mind, Lo?"

"No, I'm not, Julian. You think that acid trip stuff is so harmless I suggest you go on one yourself. You come back from it, maybe Shelley can try it. You don't, bye-bye, it's been nice knowing you."

"I'm not sure that Julian is clinically indicated for the treatment, strictly speaking, but, on the other hand, you and I both know that you still have some issues, don't you, Jules? Maybe a controlled psychedelic experience could help set you free in a sense."

"Really, Clarissa, you're going to pile on too with this ridiculous idea?"

"Well..."

Mitch, being one of the most chivalrous men alive, volunteered to do it in Julian's place, but Lois was not having it.

"Julie is the one who thinks it's such a great idea for my Shelley, so I think he should be the one to do it, but thank you,

Mitch, that was thoughtful of you. You set a fine example for my little friend here."

"Alright, alright, I'll do it, okay? Because I know if I don't do it, you'll never let it go, Lois. I'll be hearing about it for the rest of my life. Okay, I give up, I'll do it."

"Now that that's settled, we really need to discuss our decisions about the place. I know how loyal you guys are and I know you know how much this place means to me, but it's only a place. There are other places..."

"Wait, Mitch, you just said something that gave me an idea. What if we buy the piece of land across the street, really, really quickly before anyone gets wind of it, then we turn around and take the deal and get our money, then we invest our money in a new place across the street and give the Fitzgerald's a run for it."

Lois was momentarily speechless, but only momentarily.

"I got to admit that's a friggin brilliant idea, Julian. Huh!"

"I agree it's a smart strategy, Julian, but we should all be aware that Mitch's heart is here with this place."

"I'm sorry, Mitch. Maybe you'd come to love the new place the same or even more than this one?"

"Yeah, that's right, Jule, I'm sure I could get there if I had all my friends backing me up."

And so the decision was made. First they would secure the new piece of land. Then they would notify Snodgrass. The rest of the week was bitter sweet as each of the partners thought about the possibility that this or that task in service of their responsibilities at Barcus Bar and Grill would be the last. The thought of riches and the imaginary spending thereof gave some distraction but the trade-off was nonetheless depressing.

CHAPTER
Fifteen

Clarissa suggested that the time for Julian to make good on his promise had come. Shelley was not getting better, in fact, she seemed only to have gone downhill. She calculated that her client might be brightened by knowing what Julian was about to do for her. And though she was right, Shelley still foundered, such was the nature of her ism. But out of that non-communicative state she managed to push her way to the surface and insist that if Julian was doing it for her, she was doing it with him.

"Ohh, dear, your mother so wouldn't approve of that. I don't even know that when she sees Julian come out of it without a scratch she'll even keep her word about allowing you to do it."

"I'm not sure either, Clarissa, but I'm twenty-two and I'm sick of being sick and I am no longer my mother's child. I'm a grown woman and this is my decision and that is that."

"Alright, points well taken, but I'm not going to be the one to break it to Lois."

"Don't worry, no one is going to break it to Lois. Lois can deal with it after it's over and done with."

"Julian might not go along with that."

"Then, we don't need to tell him either."

"Okay. God help me if I'm screwing up here, but I think this could all work out just fine."

The deal on the land happened in record time, which was good, but then the pressure was on to give Snodgrass the go ahead, which was sticky somehow.

Tibbets and Donna's situation needed to be dealt with before the baby bump became any more pronounced so the group set off for Oyster Bay, Long Island and left Mitch and the rest of them to take care of business. The McMansion in which Donna had grown up sat at the edge of a green lawn sloping down to a cul de sac lightly populated with other such architectural monstrosities.

The Capucci men were just as beefy as Donna had described and it was a good hour before any of the entourage, Lois included, had the temerity to broach the delicate subject at hand. Donna herself was the one to finally break the ice.

"Umm, daddy, my brothers, I have something wonderful that we all came here to tell you and I think you're going to like it."

This statement brought the opposite of the hoped for warm smiles to the faces of Donna's menfolk.

"You know how you always told me that, if I was ever going to find a man, it was going to have to be a really nice and respectable and a very good, good man. Well, I did."

"You did what, cupcake?"

"I found him and he's right here, Sean Tibbets, or Tibbets like most people call him, or Tibby to me because that's how much I love him, and have been wanting for him to ask you for my hand in marriage and I guess all the rest of me too (and here Donna initiated one of her winks leaving her parent and siblings gaping and red faced) since he already asked me and my answer was already yes."

It was many hours later that the group emerged in considerably poorer shape than that in which they had arrived. Donna had managed to fill a couple of dish towels with ice as they were taking their leave. These were applied to an eye each of Julian and Tibbets respectively. Lois did the driving.

The following week. Donna and Tibbets' nuptials were announced in the local paper. By the time the actual wedding took place, several weeks after that, the bride was overjoyed to see her father and brothers arrive for the ceremony at Barcus Bar and Grill looking awkward and abnormally timid in their dress suits.

Meanwhile, Julian's heroics in dealing with the Capuccis hadn't had the desired effect of getting Lois off his case regarding the LSD. Clarissa had confirmed receipt of the relevant illicit substance and seemed to think sooner was just as good as later.

Lois preferred sooner.

Julian was surprised to see Shelley on hand as Clarissa guided him to the field near Mitch's house where he had found her happily tripping away not so many weeks before. The day was unusually warm for January, but not too warm for there to be a light snow carpeting the crusty peaks of prior winter downfalls. He wore warm clothes and comfortable boots as per instructions from his 'spirit guide.'

"Here goes nothing," he said as he tossed back the psychedelic.

"My parents would love to have seen this!"

Little did Julian know when he made that pronouncement that, in fact, his parents would pay him a visit during his trip. His parents, the Jehovah's Witnesses from his youth, his grandmother and grandfather and, oddly enough, 'My name is Chessie.' Each in turn seemed to be but passive observers.

They neither judged him nor appeared particularly distracted by what he was trying to tell them. He himself wasn't quite sure what he was trying to tell them either and he decided that it was probably not very important anyway. It was nice to see them, sort of. It was nice to not care what they thought of him.

Shelley was there and she was more beautiful than he had ever seen her and he danced with her or around her or at least he was pretty sure he did.

At some point, he found himself inside, trying to take his scarf and jacket and gloves off. He was warm, too warm. He could have sworn Clarissa was chasing him back out the door.

"Put your coat on, Jules, you'll catch a cold," he heard her say, andm for some reason, he thought this was one of the funniest things he had ever heard anyone say and he ran and swooped and fell down in the snow and picked himself back up, leaning as he did on the pool cue in his hand and holding it first as a torch and then as a spear and hollering joyfully all the way to Lois paddle tennis court.

There, he collapsed in a corner. Then, he saw Clarissa approaching and Shelley and Lois and Tirana and Mitch and Donna and Tibbets, and he stood up and placed both hands strategically on the pool stick and started charging toward the paddle tennis net and vaulted himself above the 'crowds' and landed on his feet for a second until they slid out from under him and he was flat on his back. The cheers were thunderous or so he imagined.

There had been no "Julian, if you so much as hurt a thread of my tennis net." Or "Jules, watch out, man." Or "Julian be careful." Or "Mr.D, don't do it!" No, there was none of that, only a chorus of wondrous approval, support and admiration. He had done it, he was a pole vaulter and life would never be the same.

Part of what wasn't the same was Julian not being ambulatory for the next couple of weeks. He would be the best man on crutches at the kids' wedding and the bartender on wheels at work. More importantly, though, he had a girlfriend and the girlfriend had him and there was nothing Lois could do or say about it, and though she gave as hard a time to both of them as she possibly could, she did seem to be coming around. Seeing her daughter happy went a long way toward winning her over. And she had never ever seen her daughter quite so happy.

"You think she's manic?" she asked Clarissa. "No, Lo, she's not manic, she's in love."

"You sure?"

"I know the difference."

The day after Julian's trip and considering that they had closed their land deal, the partners prepared to meet with Snodgrass and give him the green light. Mitch was the face of a man trying to rise above his somber feelings and pretend to be cheerful. Julian and Lois registered this and added it to the heaviness of their own misgivings. They all wondered how they could ever hope to duplicate the magic that had been Barcus Bar and Grill.

"Why's everyone so mopey, what's going on?" Shelley asked as she sat down in the booth next to Julian.

"Snodgrass will be here in like half an hour," Julian said.

"Well, I thought you guys were all good with your decision."

"What time is it?" Lois asked.

"The time, Mother Dear, is twenty minutes to ten, if my Apple Watch is to be trusted. And guess what else I found on my Apple Watch last night."

"Honestly, honey, nobody really cares about your Apple Watch at the moment," Lois said.

"Oh, I think you're all going to care very much about what this Apple Watch has to say. Remember, this used to be Doreen's Apple Watch before you so generously gave it to me, Mom."

"Well, go ahead," Clarissa encouraged.

Shelley turned up the volume on her watch and played back a recording on which all gathered could recognize their own voices and Snodgrass voice, The meeting wherein he revealed his entire scheme and admitted to selling Lois a bill of goods was preserved for posterity.

"I bet Fitz the IV would be very interested in hearing this. And that's not all. I have text messages that prove not only was Doreen two timing you, Mitch, but she was doing it with Snodgrass in exchange for him expunging her criminal record, the shoplifting and such."

"Sweetpea," Mitch said to Clarissa, "please call Snodgrass and tell him we need to postpone."

Fitz IV did not know what to make of Julian's offer to meet. But he figured things couldn't possibly get worse than they already were so why not.

Lois wanted to come too and Shelley and Mitch and Clarissa as well, but Julian thought it was important to take this one solo. Meet Fitz IV man to man. It was arranged that Fitz IV would pick Julian up at the bar and they'd park across the street under a stand of trees on what was now Julian and the others' property.

Secrecy was of the essence as Snodgrass had recently been known to show up unannounced in order to brow beat his reluctant clients into taking the 'deal of a lifetime.'

"Well, hello, Julian. This is something of a surprise I must confess, but you're looking well, my friend, apart from the crutches and all. Hey, that why you called me here, old mate, to show me that you are still suffering the consequences of the school trip debacle? No need, you see, my father has come to an arrangement with your charming attorney and, as far as I know, given that my family no longer communicates with me, really, we are done."

"I'm sorry to hear that, Fitz."

"So it's Fitz now, no more of that nice honorific with which you once so kindly addressed me; well what else did I expect? I'm not a particularly well-respected man at the moment. I've tried to be a gentleman, I've tried to keep it on the up and up and I nearly succeeded, my friend. The school was going along quite well. I don't think my father thought I had it in me. I felt a certain degree of newfound, what shall we call it, appreciation, goodwill, dare I say, genuine affection from the old goat. Ahh well, such is the lot of man that the sun may shine upon him one day only to rain down adversity the next. What? Am I right?"

"Fitz, let's just start by saying I'm not about to add to that rain of adversity you're talking about, but to help make that sun come back and shine on you again. With my help, you can go to your family with the means to settle this thing at half of what they thought they were going to have to pay to get you off the hook. Of course, Barcus Bar and Grill would remain in the hands of its original owners, but still we're talking about a huge cash savings."

"God bless your kind soul, my man, but don't toy with me; I've had quite enough of feeling like the proverbial donkey's ass, if you follow my meaning. That said, a desperate fellow must suffer fools and foolishness aplenty. Go ahead, then, and let me in on these so-called redemptive measures of yours."

"Well, you know Snodgrass has a recording of you right? But we have a recording of Snodgrass now, and it's the sort of recording that could put a member of the bar behind bars, if you know what I mean..."

When Fitz dropped Julian off an hour later, Snodgrass's Camaro was parked in front. Julian figured there really wasn't any need to hide anymore. The deed was done as far as the Fitzgerald were concerned. Fitz IV would get back to them later today. It was now time to let Snodgrass in on how badly he was screwed.

Needless to say, he didn't take it well. And so Fitz IV was somewhat restored in his father's eyes, at least ten million dollars worth. His younger brother, having had to give up buying Barcus Bar and Grill, looked to buy the property across the street and had to come hat in hand to Mitch when he discovered what had transpired. Mitch apologized sincerely, but assured him the property was not for sale.

With the new-found cash. The partners agreed to renovate Barcus Bar and Grill, increasing the size of the parking lot, adding a terrace for outdoor dining in the summer and getting an official valet booth for Manny and his workers.

Lois and Tirana were the first to build a home on the property across the street. Mitch and Clarissa would follow suit and rent out the house in back of the bar to the newlyweds and their infant baby girl. Julian and Shelley would bunk with Tirana and Lois until they too tied the knot and put up a house of their own. Julian reflected that maybe commune living was in his bloodstream after all. Everybody waited for Barcus and Sonia to slow down some, but that wasn't happening. A crosswalk was petitioned for and granted mostly for the purpose of getting the two of them safely across the street. Snodgrass's last bill was paid in full and he was rumored to have been spotted in Vegas working as a chaplain at one of those get married quick places.

As part of the arrangement with Fitz IV, Lois got her old job back with a pay raise and an unlimited volleyball net budget. It was nice seeing her off to work each day and getting on without her constant scrutiny Julian was not alone in thinking.

According to an occasional Disney postcard addressed to Shelley, her only friend, Doreen managed to stay sober and hold on to her Snow White job. In fact, she was dating one of the dwarfs and was proud to distinguish him as "a real dwarf, not like your husband, no offense, tee-hee."

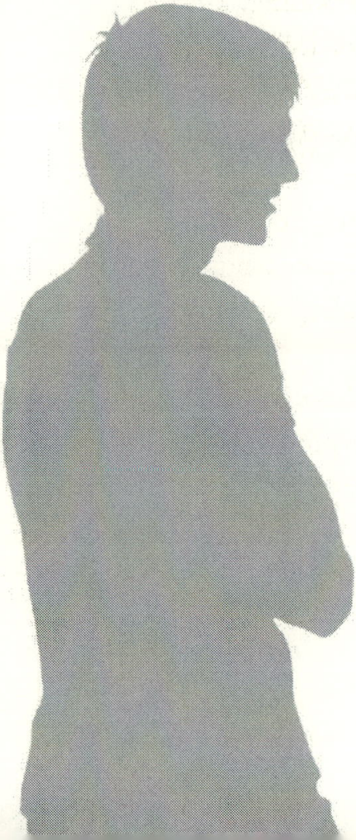

ACKNOWLEDGMENTS

To Pam and the women of the late Betsey Hotel Writers Group this story would never have been told without your kind ears and gentle prodding. Thanks too to the aforesaid Betsey, the greater part of this book was written in the wee hours in the comfy lounge off Washington Avenue that is your back lobby. What a great place to find quiet as each day hummed to a start in Miami Beach.

Thx Mom for the love of the written word you passed on to me. Thanks my second grade teacher at Oyster Bay Public School. Thanks brother Chris for always reading and always offering helpful advice.

To all of my beautiful family and all of my beautiful friends, thank you, thank you. I love making things up but what would I have to make it with and who would I have to make it for if not for you?

And, not least, thanks to Life to Paper for bringing my paper to life.

ABOUT THE AUTHOR

"It's an exclusive club - everyone's invited" is the mission and mantra of Jo Ferrone. A born rebel of eight siblings, she is best known as the co-creator of *Angela Anaconda* and **Fido Dido**, her homage to the ordinary humans living extraordinary lives - heroes for everyone. Drawn to explore she found her soulmates in dingy diners, cartoon creators drawing rooms and the backwoods of Oyster Bay, Long Island NY. A failed receptionist with abysmal typing skills, she nonetheless writes novels that reveal people as perfectly imperfect as we are. Her first book, a tale of a girl who turns into a PB&J sandwich before being eaten by a horse is of course, a 2nd grade masterpiece found only in her public school library. She resides in Miami, FL on the beach with an entourage of animal companions… and wouldn't have it any other way.

LIFE TO PAPER
PUBLISHING INC.

Life to Paper Publishing Inc. (Life to Paper) is an independent publishing house, which helps diverse, mission-driven, heart-centred individuals put their life to paper and reach and inspire audiences and readers.

Life to Paper takes a unique approach to publishing, providing not only ghostwriting, editing and hybrid-publishing services, but also marketing, branding and public relations services, to help individuals take their story from "book I wrote once" to bestseller.

Thanks to our team and partners, we are able to distribute books worldwide that touch the lives and hearts of readers. We guide our authors to discover their unique gifts and empower them to start delivering these talents to the world, therefore, achieving their dream come true and beyond.

Life to Paper aims to allow others to see an author's deepest truths that guide them on a journey to stare directly into their own. We foster storytellers because we believe that "your story can be someone's spark", and change a life.

The Bookshop by Life to Paper is a physical bookstore, which serves the community of Buena Vista, Miami, Florida. We decided to open our doors even further, supporting local authors and artists and providing a place for future authors to commence working on their stories and workshop their pieces through our literary society. The Bookshop by Life to Paper is a place of inspiration and community, showcasing that, if you set your mind to it, you can write the book of your dreams, and we'll help you along the way.

Life to Legacy Foundation is Life to Paper Publishing's not-for-profit organization dedicated to educating and empowering individuals with courses, books and resources to write their life stories. We believe we can change the world one story at a time, and the Life to Legacy Foundation is our way of giving back to all the communities that deserve to have their stories shared.

Made in United States
Orlando, FL
08 January 2022